I0772719

Upon
the Arrival of
Dawn

By Joseph Schiller

ISBN 979-8-9860275-0-0

Printed in the United States of America

1st English Edition

Contributions
Editing: Nick Stead
Book Design and Layout: Morgan Giuge

Publisher
Joseph A. Schiller
jaschiller1979@gmail.com
http://josephschiller.weebly.com
facebook.com/UpontheArrivalofDawn

To my most dedicated support.
My wife, Cinthy.

"...tasked with keeping a list, a list of names of all souls born of Earth, books of names ad infinitum[2]. Dost thou hear thy name called upon faint whispers in the night? Be thus not afraid, for ye shall receive everlasting peace, and the gods shall hence know thee once again. 'Tis time the divine servant of Heaven erased thy name promptly from the annals of existence. Upon thy brow shall he place his right hand. And his name is Death, thy escort to the beyond."

Papyrus Scroll of Unknown Origin - 2nd Century BCE[3]

Chapter 1

"The winter of one's life can be, and generally is, difficult to accept, especially when one is fully aware of just how quickly one's twilight is approaching, as is often the case in old age. The associated anxiety can be particularly acute if one is agonizing over how significantly afflicted they are in the body and mind, and therefore, how accelerated their eventual deterioration shall be. Why is this thus? It is because *death*, as a state or condition of being, is what ultimately defines mankind's mortality, determining man's terrestrial destiny. Wicked and righteous souls alike fear its gradual approach. Anyone that proclaims they are prepared for the end of their corporeal existence is either deceiving themselves or is trying to fool others.

Perhaps it is unfair for the benevolent, the righteous, to feel any trepidation. After all, did they not try to live their lives in accordance with some commonly accepted sets of principles and values, cornerstones of a virtuous life? These individuals, if any beings at all, should be able to stare off into the beyond with stout hearts, possessing confidence that their post-terrestrial circumstance will be all they believed it could be. Nevertheless, they do not. For most, death's embrace is felt the same, regardless of one's individual merit. And that feeling is trepidation."

✷✷✷✷✷✷✷✷✷

"Kah, kah, kah...kah, kah, kah!" coughed Cyril, in one of the increasingly frequent early morning spasms he had been having. "Kah, kah!"

If these spells would subside for even a moment, I might actually get a moment of peaceful slumber, he thought to himself in frustration. He was beginning to stir uncomfortably about his bed, clenching his fists around as much bedding as he could grab. The fits were becoming much more severe and persistent as of late, a source of growing concern.

While Cyril is an older gentleman, until very recently one might argue that he had enjoyed remarkably good health for a man of his advanced age. For the past several weeks, though, he had been essentially confined to his bed, unable to shake a spell of something respiratory in nature. Cyril's condition began to change innocently enough – an early winter chill of sorts – but quickly progressed further into something much more serious. Bedridden, his physical state gradually worsened to the point that his family felt obligated to step in to tend to him full time.

When the family's collective efforts to help him overcome his ailing condition failed, several physicians were dispatched to attempt to diagnose and treat him, all to no discernible avail. At the same time, the family, as is the wont of most of mankind when faced with similar circumstances, turned more of their attention toward a deity upon which they projected all of their collective hope could and or would intervene on their behalf, and make their loved one whole once again. While hopeful, there were some members of Cyril's extended family who, nevertheless, began preparing for what seemed inevitable – their patriarch's passing. And so, the family sought the presence of men they believed could intercede spiritually.

Mankind's view of its physical condition early in life seems often to be one of almost invincibility or infallibility. Death, however, tends to remind all of just how truly fragile the nature of cellular organisms really is. Cyril's family could regrettably only sit in earnest vigil day and night, while hoping desperately for signs that his situation would improve.

Cyril's comfort was looked upon with the utmost care and absolute dedication. No expenses or conveniences were spared in providing for what was increasingly expected to be the family elder's last days, or perhaps hours. If only everyone in such a state could be looked after with such an unconditional outpouring of compassion and devotion.

A man beloved by all that had the pleasure of knowing him, Cyril was, as would be considered by most, a *good* man. While he led, by all accounts, an unassuming and arguably ordinary life, he was at the same time virtuous and not without a sort of merit in humility.

Cyril was not an overly recognizable figure within or without his community any more than others of moderate success in life tend to be. As far as greater mankind is concerned with acquiring more money or possessions throughout life, he was by no means categorically wealthy. Nevertheless, he was, and it must be emphasized, more than respected by the few lucky enough to call him family, friend, and acquaintance.

Prior to this most recent period in Cyril's life, of which this tale begins, Cyril was merely a humble clockmaker, constructing and repairing various time pieces in his small shop below the set of family apartments just a few paces from the center of his village. Certainly not a trade of any glamor or notoriety, but working hard, he was able to afford a sufficiently comfortable livelihood for his modestly sized family. Cyril was a good provider and a man adored by all. Now his family and friends were repaying his love and kindness in turn, with their own adoration.

✳ ✳ ✳ ✳ ✳ ✳ ✳ ✳ ✳ ✳

Cyril's hacking subsided long enough to allow him to gradually breathe a bit more steadily, and with a little less effort. He slowly opened his eyelids, and, with tremendous anguish, sat himself up in his bed. In his feeble condition he usually required someone's assistance in order to move his fragile frame in any small way. He forced himself on this occasion out of a sudden sense of necessity. His numerous bedsores, a constant source of discomfort, were beginning to irritate him again, making the skin on his underside raw and sensitive to the touch. Gathering what little strength he could, Cyril propped himself up on his elbows.

Gingerly rotating his head about, Cyril slowly scanned his modest room. He noticed a small bowl of food was set carefully upon the nightstand next to his bed-chamber. By the appearance of its contents, it was some sort of porridge, and had most likely been there for a while.

Cyril knew his wife had been in to see him at some point earlier in the evening. The porridge by now had likely lost any aroma or flavor.

Food was once such an indulgence, though, now he was reduced to a largely liquid diet. In fact, he often had to force himself to consume whatever was prepared and act grateful for it. He stared at the bowl for several minutes, unable to decide whether he was desperate enough to try eating, before being overcome once again with sluggishness.

Fatigue often quickly evolved into drowsiness. Gently laying back down in bed, straining just as much as he had when he sat up, Cyril closed his eyes in an effort to return to sleep. In his heart, he said a quick prayer, asking in desperation for uninterrupted slumber; something he had not enjoyed now for several weeks.

He had just started to drift off when something startled him back to reality, believing that he had heard something faint, something akin to a soft voice calling out in the darkness of his bedroom. Heart thumping almost out of his chest, he remained perfectly motionless, holding his breath as best he could as he strained his ears for a hint of what had woken him. After several moments of no perceptible noise of any kind, Cyril felt convinced that he was in fact mistaken.

After all, this old home always makes such unex-

plainable noises, Cyril thought to himself.

It was possible that one of the many guests that had recently visited had perhaps neglected to close a window before retiring from the bedroom. Slightly frustrated with the prospect of being kept up all night with the constant swishing and swaying from an evening breeze stirring the curtains about his chambers, Cyril closed his eyes once again with a renewed determination to get a few more hours of repose before something else jolted him awake.

These thoughts of rest had no sooner filled his mind than Cyril once again thought he heard the faint call penetrating the silence ever so softly. This time, however, the voice seemed to be speaking his name, as a gentle whisper into one's ear. With all of the intensity that he could gather, Cyril listened for the voice to repeat itself. His mind and heart began to race once again, renewed with scattered thoughts. Was this perceived voice merely the imaginings of a sick man? He was never one that believed in ghosts or specters, but he found himself questioning how firmly he disbelieved. He was not disappointed when several seconds later, like the passing of a light spring breeze across one's face, and yet almost entirely imperceptible, Cyril was convinced that he unmistakably heard his own name called out to him from a yet undetermined corner within his room.

"Cyril..."

"Who's there?!" Cyril called out as loudly as he could into the nothingness of the room, while nearly choking on his own words.

He was beginning to perspire quite heavily, sweat beading across his brow, while his heart rate now began to race out of control within his frail frame. He tried again to calm himself down by attempting to convince himself that the *voice* he believed that he had heard was nothing more than a symptomatic of a senile old man in desperate need of rest. After all, he was extremely sick, and anyone in his particular condition could be forgiven for having periodic episodes of delirium.

"Yes, that is precisely what I am experiencing. These are simply hallucinations brought on by my weakened condition. My poor body is so tired. The sooner my eternal rest begins, the better," Cyril declared under his breath.

His mind wandered for a few moments. The instan-taneous and equally terrifying realization that there was something like a hand resting gently on his left shoulder brought him back. "Who's there?" he called out again.

Shivers immediately passed along his nerves. Fear-ing to move even a millimeter, he kept absolutely still for what seemed an eternity. A steadily rising heart rate and cold sweat returned with increased intensity. Finally, Cyril collected what little courage he could and painfully tilted his head ever so slightly toward his left side, to look upon whoever or whatever had taken hold of his shoulder. His eyes, finally fully adjusted to the absence of light, rested on an unfamiliar personage positioned on his left, and Cyril's entire being frozen in debilitating shock. Terror instantly overcame him at the recognition of the figure moving to sit next to him on his bed. Terror, because he had an equally strong impression as to why this visitor was present.

This state of paralysis lasted for what felt like forever to Cyril. He feared and refused to move, to blink, to breathe, or to even make a sound. Wanting desperately to believe that he was in fact just dreaming, he tried to convince himself that at any moment something would at last stir him awake; that what he was experiencing was nothing more than a bad bout of hysteria. The personage's eyes, nevertheless, remained locked with his, neither set deviating from the other.

It was the specter that finally penetrated the silence.

"You recognize me, do you not?" whispered the figure rhetorically, with an almost inhuman voice. "You know of me and have strong suspicions of precisely why I'm here. Are you surprised?"

Despite the solicitation, Cyril made no effort to respond in any way to the prompt. While not being aware of exactly why, there was a strange and instinctive acknowledgement of this being lingering by his side. Consequently, he was beginning, intuitively, to recognize this mysterious guest's purpose for visiting, and, therefore, he remained resolved not to reply.

"It's perfectly understandable that you would resist responding," said the strange visitor in an attempt to break the stalemate.

The stranger looked upon Cyril with an almost gentle gaze, cocking his neck to the side slightly as he did. "By doing so, you believe that you would ultimately be acknowledging my presence. And, by not answering…well, what do you hope the outcome to be? As much as you would like to convince yourself that these sensations, both auditory and visual, are nothing more than the product of your weakened physical state, deep down in your core you know that is mere foolishness. Yes…I can read your thoughts, and your feelings, as I can of all of your kind."

Cyril attempted to make out the full features of this personage. While he was unable to accurately discern anything for certain, he was able to catch some vague physical traits. Yet, he was unsure whether his eyes were betraying him. Nevertheless, the being sitting at his bedside appeared to be a relatively young man, though it was hard to estimate an age. From what Cyril could recognize, his lines were soft, calm, with an almost childlike innocence. In fact, his features had an almost disarming quality to them. Cyril stared at those eyes gazing deeply into his.

It did not matter that he could not see the specter clearly. He could feel the intensity in that gaze; could feel how the specter's eyes never lost their focus for even an instant. Yet he also sensed what seemed like a friendly enough grin.

After a few seconds, when the mysterious figure was assured that Cyril was fully attentive, he continued, "Do you know why you recognize me?"

"No." It came out as a stutter, betraying the persistent state of absolute terror Cyril had found himself in.

"That is not entirely truthful, is it? You felt my presence the very instant I entered this room. Your energy flowing through you is as familiar with mine as mine is with yours, as it is with the rest of your mortal brothers and sisters. For we are all part of the same creative force, are we not? Your spirit, if you will, recognized the presence of a force, which, as it did mine, similarly created your existence," added the mysterious guest.

The specter smiled at Cyril, almost warmly. "I am sensing a heightened anxiety within you. There is no need to feel such fear. Be at peace."

There was a rather long pause before either said anything else. Cyril found it impossible to settle his heart and mind, though, not without trying. Despite the strange visitor's admonishment to remain at peace, Cyril felt strongly that those were merely convenient words.

Finally, Cyril gave in, and ventured into a conversation with all the remaining bravery available within him. "Is this the end of my time?"

With absolutely no hesitation, the voice of the specter replied in the affirmative. "Yes. Though, you already anticipated that I would answer as such."

"I suuu...suppose I dddd...did," Cyril said in the trembling tone of a man beginning to accept, and in deep contemplation of, his fate.

"Cyril, try to settle your heart and your mind," suggested the specter. "Arrangements have all been made for you."

At that moment, Cyril noticed the visitor's countenance begin to change, darkening and swelling like lengthening shadows. A sinister smile gradually formed across the visitor's face. Whatever lingering peace and calm Cyril previously had left in his heart quickly vanished and was replaced immediately with a renewed sense of anguish and horror. His first instinct was to use what fleeting strength he could muster to flee from his room in search of help, or to call out to his family elsewhere within the home. His condition, however, was simply too fragile for any attempted outburst or escape. He found it equally difficult to raise his voice much more than a whisper. Meanwhile, the personage just sat and watched him struggle, staring with an increasingly malicious look of enjoyment on his face.

The stranger then slowly rose up from his sitting position on top of the bed, and once again stood at Cyril's side. He then walked with great purpose toward the window, almost gliding as he did, before eventually taking a position at the front of the room, facing out onto the empty street below. Pausing, the figure looked out into the dark of the night, almost as if he drew strength from it. He remained thus, peering out for several minutes in deep silence. Cyril himself was too struck with fear to do anything to break that silence. It seemed that this being had been sent to escort his soul away to meet his maker. What he could not reconcile was why he felt so mortified instead of elated.

While continuing to peer out the window, the terrible figure stated, "There are several questions you have chosen, as of yet, not to ask me. Perhaps you are afraid of the responses."

It took Cyril a moment, but eventually he managed to choke out one of the questions lingering in his heart. "Am...am I going to heaven, or hell?"

The guest in Cyril's bedchamber responded with a short chuckle – a fiendish cackle. Though brief, the laugh betrayed an intensely demonic nature. "Countless ages have wrestled with such futile questions."

Cyril was beginning to think his heart would give out just from talking to this terrible specter. *Was that why the thing had come to visit? To hasten my demise?* He shuddered and the increasingly terrifying visitor laughed. He sensed that the terrible personage was deriving more pleasure from his heightened anxiety and fear.

"I have had you in mind for some time," the stranger said. "You led a life more than worthy of having the energy of your soul returned to the source, the origins of all creation, or *heaven* – the thing corporeal beings commonly refer to as the afterlife." He gave another malevolent giggle, whilst still maintaining his gaze out the window. "However, … I have other plans for your departing soul."

Cyril was once again stunned – paralyzed even – with an indescribable fright. A darkness seized upon the deepest reaches of his heart. It took him several minutes to even marginally recover his faculties.

"Whooo…. who are you?" he asked, trembling and gasping uncontrollably at this point.

Cyril was surprised when his visitor did not respond. He was about to repeat himself when he thought he heard a sudden rushing sound from outside the bedroom window; the kind of noise made by a strong gust of autumn wind. A wind, from the sound of it, was fast approaching. Turning his ear ever so slightly toward the direction of the disturbance, Cyril now thought that perhaps the noise sounded not like a wind at all, but like the beating of thousands of sets of wings, accompanied by ever louder, unexplainable shrieks. And his terror increased a thousandfold.

Suddenly, and without warning, the specter turned. Those intense eyes gleamed with malevolence as he coldly answered, "I am... the Taker of Souls!"

Without hesitation, the devilish form threw open the bedroom window in order to allow in a flood of demons; terrible spirits called Keres summoned for the purpose of devouring souls. At his bidding, the Keres quickly went to work to rip Cyril's life energy from its mortal frame. His soul screamed out in tremendous and dreadful agony, a scream that reached every conceivable corner of the time and space of Creation.

✳ ✳ ✳ ✳ ✳ ✳ ✳ ✳ ✳

Silence soon prevailed. There were no discernible traces remaining of any activity in Cyril's apartment; none, except for Cyril's cold and lifeless body lying in his bed. One might have mistaken him to be in a deep and permanent slumber, were it not for the terror of his final moments frozen in his lifeless face, the eyes staring at their tormentors and the mouth agape in a silent outburst.

Chapter 2

Cyril's bedroom, and the entirety of his home for that matter, remained absolutely still well into the early morning hours. Not a soul stirred from their evening's slumber.
Winter had begun to reveal itself in the increasing chill,
taking an ever-greater stronghold over the landscape, occasionally leaving its frosted kisses upon what had been, in
Cyril's mortality, the windowpanes of his chambers. While
the early morning sky still displayed a few remaining
stars twinkling across her firmament, a thin layer of wispy
clouds had slowly crept in and was gradually concealing
them from view. Only periodic glimpses of the marvelous
expanse were allowed. The scene would have otherwise
been described as tranquil, betraying no signs of the evil

that had transpired earlier.

✳✳✳✳✳✳✳✳✳

Another shadowy figure appeared at the foot of Cyril's bed, taking long, deep breaths, and gazing at length at the deceased man's cold remains as they lay eternally motionless on top of a crumpled mess of sheets. The figure rested his hands gently upon the footboard, gripping lightly while periodically rubbing the palms of his hands along the smooth lacquered grain of the wooden frame, almost as if coming in contact with the texture of the furniture produced some entirely new sensation that this visitor had not yet had the pleasure of experiencing. The stranger's glances slowly shifted, starting at Cyril's bed frame and moving about the small room, scanning the scene methodically, fixating at moments, only to return again to scanning. No corner of the room was overlooked; every point was given equal attention and scrutinized thoroughly. After making a quick, yet careful, study of the surroundings, he stepped around to the right side of the bed, pausing alongside Cyril's corpse.

Leaning down towards Cyril's remains, the stranger lifted and placed his right hand gently upon the corpse's forehead, rubbing it ever so delicately several times. The warmth that Cyril's mortal body at one time possessed no longer radiated through these carbon remnants. The figure continued this rubbing action for several minutes, looking down on the deceased, full of sincerity and tenderness. Were someone to be in the room to witness the scene, they would not be blamed for believing the mysterious guest to be an intimate friend. The mysterious guest's countenance soon changed, however, to one of grave concern, even deep distress. His clairvoyance enabled him to begin to assemble the timeline of events that had taken place prior to his arrival. The preliminary evidence that could be derived suggested that someone, or more correctly, something, had claimed and consumed the energy that once animated Cyril's form. If confirmed, this could possibly suggest that a cosmic essence, or essences, had violated their sacred charge, and thus the holy celestial creed itself. Such a circumstance raised numerous, disturbing questions, and posed difficult quandaries for the visitor; questions for which, he recognized, answers must be gathered in great haste.

The visitor began moving once again about the bedchamber, patiently, methodically, as if he were a detective of sorts, attempting to sniff out clues left behind at a crime scene. He felt strongly that he should look over the apartment once more. Every little detail, even the seemingly insignificant, drew the stranger's full and undivided attention. A casual observer to the scene would not have noticed anything out of the ordinary; yet this figure was meticulous because he was not seeking out purely physical evidence, but more specifically, he sought the ethereal echoes left behind, which are only perceptible by a select set of essences.

The Ethereal Echo, or the continual trail left behind by any and all cosmic disturbances, is the ongoing record of that which has, is, and will take place at any given moment in time and space across this vast expansive universe[4]. These reverberations are like instantaneous snapshots along the timelines of the Cosmos. The energy signatures of all living beings are constantly embroidering the fabric of space and time with the moments of their existences. The stranger scanned the apartment for those very signs of what had taken place with great purpose and intention. What unraveled before him disturbed him considerably more than he could have ever imagined in all his endless centuries of existence.

What the being was able to gradually puzzle together was an event of unspeakable wickedness; one in which Cyril suffered a horrendous fate. A soul that was once destined to have its life energy promptly and honorably returned to the state of original creation upon its eventual demise, was prematurely eliminated, devoured by damned spirits, and thus placed in an eternal limbo, enslaved to become a servant of evil itself. The outsider could not understand why something so dastardly had happened, baffling any attempt to formulate a coherent explanation. Clearly, Keres[5] had been present, and were guilty of the atrocities he was now obliged to investigate. Nevertheless, the *why* and *what* behind the act were entirely unclear, and were, therefore, the most disturbing aspects of the forthcoming investigation.

The transient entity sat himself down for a moment on a chair in a far corner of the room, trying to process everything. He asked himself again what might have been behind such an act, as was revealed to him by the Ethereal Echo. For the Keres would not and could not devour the soul of someone of the physical plane without having been directed to do so first by a divine servant, whose duty was to escort wicked souls into the cosmic abyss beyond nothingness. Even if this was what had occurred, it must be a mortal deemed to be evil in order for a cosmic agent and Keres to be involved. For it was this mysterious visitor's responsibility and directive, and his alone, to help the souls of the righteous by escorting them to a reunification of the energy of life with that of Creation. He would have escorted Cyril to the afterlife when the properly designated time was determined by the Universe to be Cyril's end. Something, therefore, directed the Keres to ravish the soul of a righteous being against the Law of Eternity, suggesting unfathomable ideas for the mysterious companion.

What made this scene even more disturbing was not just the gruesome or questionable nature of what was recorded in the Ethereal Echo. On the contrary, this was not the first such instance; the stranger was aware of evidence suggesting similar incidents where righteous souls had been devoured by the Keres; and these were occurring with increasing frequency across Existence. The increase was so alarming that it began to lead the guest, a being generally above earthly feelings of fear and anxiety, to become marginally frightened by what this increasing evil implied. All that could be surmised thus far was that there had clearly been a stirring presence of malevolence about the terrestrial realm – an unjust proportion of wickedness.

The mysterious personage, while making one final pass around the small confines of Cyril's bedroom, vowed to himself, and the sacred office which he faithfully held, to get to the bottom of the mystifying deaths of so many decent souls.

"I, Azrael, the divinely ordained Escort of Righteous Souls, will hunt down whichever essence is responsible for causing such a dangerous imbalance between good and evil in the Universe, and bring about justice throughout the Cosmos!"[6] he promised to himself as he finally departed the scene. "It is I, and only I, that has been chosen on high to retrieve the souls of righteous creatures, and usher them back to be connected once again with the energy of all Creation. This sacred responsibility is not to be trifled with." He spoke with such conviction; it was as if the very shadows quivered before him.

✶✶✶✶✶✶✶✶✶

There was once a time, recorded in the annals of the Cosmos, when the essence known as Azrael was much more than just an usher of deceased souls.[7] At one point along the Universe's infinite timeline, Azrael was one of the chosen sons of Creation; a member of the Council of Light, or Seraphim Council. Despite his elevated station as an immortal lord of Eternity, he had one weakness – his feelings for a mortal woman. Azrael had succumbed to her charms, a strict violation of the Law of Dissonance. Charges were brought to the Council of Light, and Azrael was ultimately cast out of the Council, having been found guilty of violating the Law of Dissonance. Therefore, it was determined that his essence should be reduced to inhabit a terrestrial, and thus, imperfect, body – the very form which had brought about his fall to begin with. The first part of his eternal punishment was that he should have to live out a mortal existence, to experience all of the pain, suffering, and struggle therewith.

Azrael would live out his human experience with

the mortal woman with whom he had fallen in love, and the son they had conceived together. He gained some small degree of recognition as a humble, yet accomplished physician, trying desperately to help his beloved terrestrials cheat death.[8]

After growing old among the mortal races he so adored, Azrael suffered to feel the throes of death himself before ultimately returning to Creation. It was then that the Council handed down the final portion of his punishment. It was determined that Azrael was to serve the needs of Creation for eternity. His essence was sentenced to collect the passing souls of mortal beings and return them to the energy of all Cosmic beginnings, thus completing his humiliation, for his shame would forever be his intimacy with mortal suffering and death; to experience all of the anguish, loss, and fear with that most sorrowful of sacraments. When the names of terrestrial beings across the Universe are read in the halls of Eternity from the Tablet of Destiny, or Cosmic Record, Azrael must hasten the call to collect those spirit's home.

For Eternity Azrael will continue to serve out penance. With the sacred power, the Word of Death[9] bestowed upon him for the purpose of fulfilling his sentence and allowing him dominion over the terrestrial plane of existence, Azrael is thus able to move freely between Creation and the created.[10]

Chapter 3

In the deepening of twilight, standing motionless under the cover of a second-floor awning during a late evening downpour, Azrael gazed lazily off at a short distance. He had positioned himself just a few yards away from, and across, a very narrow cobblestone lane from a rather humble and quiet unassuming home. There was nothing remarkable about the structure or its half-timber exterior facade. There were hundreds just like it in this village. Azrael paid very little attention to much of what he saw at all, for his focus was on something else entirely.

Not a single person could be seen strolling about the neighborhood; there were absolutely no signs of life outdoors. Azrael was, therefore, allowed to go completely unnoticed for the whole while he took up position in the passageway. As was common during such poor weather conditions and the time of evening, the townspeople of the community chose to remain comfortable indoors; preferring to stay dry, and relatively close to the remaining coals from the cooking fire in the hearth for warmth. Despite being a late summer evening, the rain shower caused the temperature to fall considerably. One might even say it was chilly. Though Azrael was not affected by temporal sensations such as the temperature in the air, he did consider how pleasant the night had become as a result of the shower passing through. Rain, he thought to himself, always has a wonderful cleansing effect. Being immortal did not prevent Azrael from fully recognizing, and thus, appreciating, the various wonders of Creation.

Despite the absence of all sources of light outside, his relative distance from the home, and the increasingly heavy downpour, Azrael was able to clearly peer into one of the small second-story windows which faced out onto the street. Roughly half a dozen candles sat on the windowsills, flickering as they illuminated the confines of the apartment within, just enough for those present inside. He was able to sufficiently observe an extremely emotional vigil surrounding a dying member of their family, the matriarch of the household. A dozen or so loved ones had taken up various positions around the deathbed and, throughout the humble room of the soul soon to depart, the gathering displayed the full range of common emotion one might expect on such a somber occasion.

The visitor did not wish to draw attention to himself, and he was very purposeful about remaining completely inconspicuous. Nevertheless, he did intend to maintain his watch over the home, confident that no one would disturb him while thus doing so.

For several hours Azrael stood patiently, never diverting his gaze for even a fraction of a moment from the dying woman's chambers, or her devoted family members and friends still lingering by her side. He stood long enough that the rain had time to start and stop several times before stopping completely, and the rain clouds eventually moved off, revealing in their departure a brilliant night sky full of sparkling stars.

Back inside the modest bedroom in which the withered remains of the mortal being lay, the family and friends in attendance continued as they had for much of the last several days, devotedly and patiently waiting in unbearable anxiety for the inevitable, which would be their matriarch's last moment on this mortal plane. A great many prayers were offered, wonderful memories were told and retold again, warm tears were shed, and feelings of tremendous sadness were shared. Azrael reminisced that such scenes, as was his privilege to have witnessed over the vastness of infinite space and time, rarely differed in any discernible way from each other. Regardless, he noted to himself that the deep emotions expressed in these final moments of mortal man's physical life were some of the most precious aspects of serving in the terrestrial realm. So intense could those feelings be that Azrael felt each experience with them only served to tie him down further with yet another chord of sympathy.

While a few guests visited only for a final moment with the dying woman, those closest to her remained consistent figures around the home. Some occupied themselves as they could; attending to their dying beloved, preparing sustenance for those present, or simply sitting about in the foolish hope that by being present circumstances would somehow miraculously improve. It was such that the scene remained for some time deep into the evening hours.

✳✳✳✳✳✳✳✳✳✳

"How cruel death must seem to corporeal beings, to live such a relatively short period of time only to have that experience in existence terminated after having seemingly just begun. I have overheard the thoughts of millions of creatures asking, '"What is the purpose of having been created, or even living, if only to have that life extinguished in the end? What is the greater meaning of life?'" What mankind does not realize, through no fault of their own, is that those are the wrong questions. What these simple beings should be asking themselves is, "'Is Creation bound by such notions as *purpose* or *meaning*?'" The answer is *no*. *Purpose* and *meaning* are cognitive constructs developed by creatures that have no basis or means to fully comprehend the spectacular mysteries of the Cosmos and want desperately to know those answers. Unfortunately, in their desperation, any reasonable answer at all will satisfy them. Creation simply is.

"Intelligent beings of every part of the Universe have developed various belief systems, explanations, theories, and mythologies in an attempt to try in some way to formulate a coherent understanding of Creation and the greater Cosmos. Each terrestrial organism, for its part, inherently feels an unmistakable connection with the collective energy from which it was once conceived, and, therefore, each being seeks to understand exactly what that connection is. Over the millennia, some have claimed to speak with, or on behalf of, deities, or a deity, in the form of divine revelation as some kind of chosen messenger. Others have proclaimed they have the guidance of a holy spirit, or a visiting angel. All such people, however, are, without realizing it, misguided by their longing for answers and, in some unfortunate cases, a foolish desire to deceive others with false promises about the nature of Existence. Existence simply is.

"It is at death that mortal entities will finally come face to face with the ultimate reality that their terrestrial existence is in reality a collection of energies that, together, combine to constantly create new Life. A mortal creature's death is only a continuation of life.[11] The Cosmos is an agglomeration of raw energy. Combined, that energy is Creation, and Creation is the foundation of Existence. Man is nothing more than a byproduct of the random output of Existence. Upon death, the energy that, at one time, sustained the life of a person returns to the source of all of that energy: the Cosmos. The energies of the universe have always been, always are, and always will be. The Cosmos simply is.

"If the creatures across Existence could fully comprehend their infinitesimally small part in the greater Cosmic cycle, perhaps they would cease occupying their hearts and minds with nonsense, and instead choose to live the short period they have in existence accordingly. They are all part of something inexplicably remarkable."

✳✳✳✳✳✳✳✳✳

It was very early in the morning before the faithfully watchful family members finally began to retire. They were clearly exhausted from the prolonged period of attentiveness. One by one they found some place to eventually lie down for a few hours of rest. Azrael, for his part, continued to wait patiently, as he had all the previous evening long, for the room of the dying woman to clear of its guests.

Once Azrael could be sure the room was completely vacant, he transported himself within, taking up a position, as was his custom, at the foot of the bed frame of the mortal body soon to be deceased. Azrael stood still, choosing simply to gaze longingly upon the frail frame of the departing woman, acknowledging to himself how genuinely gentle she was as a person, and how wholesome she had lived her life.

As the remaining clouds in the sky continued to move off after having shed the last of their tears, the brilliant light of the moon increasingly shone down upon the beautiful city. A portion of that radiant moonlight crept through the windows of the apartment which had hitherto been the focus of so much of Azrael's attention, illuminating it just enough to make candlelight no longer necessary. The dear dying woman's body lay in a dull glow, the surreal effect of the moonlight reflecting off her increasingly pale skin. Azrael thought to himself, *Soon, my dearest creature, you will be privileged to reunite with that very light shining in on you right now, returning to the glorious energy from which your kind sprang. I cannot help but envy the eternal rest for which your existence will soon begin.*

✱✱✱✱✱✱✱✱✱✱

Soon there was the faintest of stirrings within the bed. The dying woman began to show signs, almost unnoticeable at first, of waking from what had been a deep slumber. Had the family members in residence at the time been aware of this recent activity of their loved one, they would certainly not have believed their own senses. Their beloved matriarch had been virtually unresponsive for several days straight, demonstrating no visible hints of life aside from a very faint breath. Initially, it was nothing more than a mere twitch of a finger. Eventually, however, the woman was gently tossing and turning about. Her general awareness increased with each passing moment of wakefulness.

Choosing initially to keep her eyes closed for the time being, while continuing to gradually adjust to consciousness, she tilted her right ear ever so slightly toward the center of the room.

What was that sound?, she asked herself as she struggled to listen into the silence. She believed firmly that a noise of some kind was indeed responsible for waking her. *It must have been something,* she thought. There was also a sudden, yet unmistakably pleasant feeling of calm and peace that was slowly inching over her.[12] She continued to wonder to herself, however, *What had been so powerful as to disturb me out of such a state as this?*

No, she told herself. *It must be nothing of consequence, nothing more than commotion caused by one of the many family members that I've faintly perceived coming and going.*

At that very instant, the woman thought she caught another faint sound of an inaudible whisper reaching out to her from a corner across the room. She could not clearly differentiate, of course, whether she actually heard something or if, rather, she instead felt something. Perhaps she was experiencing both sensations simultaneously. Then, it transpired once again, though this time a little more pronounced and distinguishable than before.

"Maria..."

While she fully conceded that she could quite possibly have just been suffering from poor perception, especially in her state of occasional delirium, it was becoming more and more obvious to the dying matriarch that she was in fact hearing her name. And yet there was no way that was possible.

"Maria..." her name seemed to be called out, periodically. After several minutes of listening solely for the source of the mysterious whisper, she opened her eyes, struggling awkwardly at first, but eventually gaining the full optical exposure of her surroundings. She had hoped that her eyes, though failing in old age as they were, might be able to help her marginally identify the source of the as yet unidentifiable voice that she believed she was hearing.

Who is calling out my name? Her gaze continued to dart about the room as best as she could in her fragile condition in the near complete darkness, taking her time to catch every corner of the room. Nevertheless, she was forced to come to the initial conclusion that there was no one and nothing in the room.

"Maria..."

Fear now began to rise within the gentle frame of the dying woman. The vocalization, if it could even be categorized as such, was being carried across the room like a light breeze on a late summer evening, each time varying in intensity.

"Maria..."

Maria began to feel compelled by some force to call back toward the general direction of the mysterious voice. She struggled at first for the strength to even slightly move her lips. Despite the initial difficulty, however, she eventually found the necessary strength to adequately articulate a simple question. In a low, almost raspy voice, Maria finally allowed herself to ask, "Who calls my name?"

Maria waited for a few moments, though it felt like

an eternity to her, for some reply. When she did not get one, she struggled once again to repeat herself. This time, she attempted to project her voice a little bit more. "Who is there? Who calls my name?"

These words had barely left her thin, shriveled lips when Maria had the sudden sensation that there was now someone or something lingering in the silence, off in the empty space of her small bedroom. She toiled with a lack of vigor for several seconds while at the same time trying to string together a sequence of coherently clear sounds in her throat and form them into a question. Her lips quivered uncontrollably as she asked, "Who are you?"

The good woman, despite the almost overwhelming anxiety bubbling in her bosom, was just about to repeat herself once again when she abruptly caught sight of an unknown personage beginning to take slow, steady, gliding steps forward toward the far corner of her bed frame. The stranger made absolutely no reply. After a few steps, the figure simply stopped. While Maria could not be certain who or what she was peering at through the obscurity created by the darkness, she was, however, becoming more and more convinced that it was the outline of a man. Both beings stared at each other for several minutes in the dimness, each unwilling to look away from the other. Neither said a word nor made a sound.

The strange figure finally interrupted the awkward

silence. "Maria…Please do not be alarmed," he requested in a hushed tone. Maria was surprised at how genuinely warm the words felt.

A second later, the mysterious guest stepped further forward, along the side of the bed this time. When he was close enough to her, it became clear to Maria that her first impression was in fact correct – she was seeing what appeared to be the form of a young man. Maria was first overcome by how remarkably beautiful he was, this man whose face had soft, clean lines, not yet twisted and distorted by the turmoil of life. Nevertheless, there was something additional that was not totally natural about his presence, either. Her impulses were telling her that there was more to him than met the eye; something rather special.

When the mysterious man finally reached Maria's left shoulder, to the side of the bed, he paused again, then leaned over, looking directly down upon her frame. She, in turn, did her best to tilt her head as much as her frail condition would allow her to meet his gaze, looking up at the unknown guest.

"You have absolutely nothing to fear from me, dear woman," the unknown figure began again.[13] "This is a most exciting moment for you. One journey is inevitably coming to a close, while another is only just beginning. For yours has been a very special spirit, and a glorious new beginning awaits your soul."

As Maria listened to her uninvited guest speak, a feeling began to grow gradually within her heart. She felt odd, as though she intimately knew this man before her. Nay, she not only knew him, but there seemed to be much more that she could not immediately recognize. Maria stared deeply into her visitor's eyes, finding that they were effectively drawing her in somehow, revealing to her soul an answer to questions she did not as of yet even realize she had. There was in fact a very strong connection with this figure, akin to what she likened to being reunited with a long-lost friend after dozens of years spent apart.

Then, like an unexpected surge of electricity running and coursing throughout her weakened body, Maria's intuition hinted to her as to precisely who the being by her side actually was. That shiver continued to pulse throughout her limbs.[14]

There was only one way in which Maria wanted to respond to this new revelation she so profoundly felt. Only one thing occupied her mind at that immediate moment. In her thoughts, she asked herself, *Is this truly my time? Have I earned the grace and favor of my Lord?* The matriarch's eyes began to well up with moisture as she continued locked in a gaze with her visitor. That moisture quickly turned into a steady stream of warm tears running down the length of her aged face.

"Yes!" came the mysterious guest's reply, without hesitation. He then leaned closer toward Maria's infirm body, coming to within just a few inches of her now glistening, tear-covered face, and simply repeated in a gentle whisper, "Yes!"

The stranger pulled himself back. Maria recognized he was allowing her a moment, and the act of kindness only hastened her flow of tears.

The next few minutes proved to be enough for Maria to gain some measure of composure. Wiping away the remaining tears under her reddened eyes, she mustered the courage to ask her enigmatic guest, "Will you be taking me to my Lord in Heaven?" They were not the words of a woman in the twilight of her years, but those of a little girl addressing a parent. It could not go unnoticed that Maria had a bright twinkle now in her eyes. The figure turned away from the old woman, smiling to himself as he did so, then tilted his head slightly as he looked back at Maria's pale and shriveled body. Maria could not help but smile back up to him contagiously in return.

The stranger finally introduced himself. "I am called Azrael, and I have come to escort your essence back to glory!"

This revelation had a powerful effect on the dying woman. A tremendous burden and concern weighing down her spirit, as is the case with all terrestrial souls, was essentially lifted from her proverbial shoulders, never to rest upon her mind and heart again. Not once did Maria take her eyes off Azrael's. The immeasurable joy and exhilaration she now felt overpowered her. Though she tried, she could not hold back the warm tears that began to run down her face anew, in great volume. She even allowed a slight smile to crack through her otherwise somber expression, which had the effect of bringing Azrael to smile even wider.

When Maria broke the silence – after a bit of an understandable hesitation – she expressed just how elated she was. "Finally, it is my time!" she exclaimed with relief.

Maria noted how the stranger remained quiet for a short while, choosing instead to allow her an uninterrupted opportunity to open up her heart. The realization filled her with such warmth, and though she could not know it then, for Azrael, in all of the innumerable, upon innumerable deaths he was blessed to have witnessed over the infinite vastness of millennia, this was the single most rewarding part of his calling. To be a part of the moment when a corporeal being begins to find that first glimpse of eternal peace and rest for their life's energy – it brought him a joy like no other. For, though an eternal entity, these were the occasions from which he would grow more and more to appreciate Creation in its various forms and functions.

Through the steady drops of tears that were still trickling down her face, Maria added, "I often pondered what it would be like when I passed away; asking myself, more often lately, whether or not I would be ready for that moment when it came. I can honestly say now that I *am* ready. I suppose, in truth, I've been ready for some time now. There comes a time, doesn't there, in a person's life when they feel that their existence has simply run the full measure of its course. My heart is overjoyed. My moment has arrived. The only lingering thought I have is of concern for the well-being of my loved ones. Though, I suppose I'm not as much value to them as I once was. Tell me, stranger, does one's soul ever learn to cope with the loss of its family and friends? Will I have peace, despite my departure from them?"

Maria saw a smile form on Azrael's countenance as she spoke. She could almost somehow sense Azrael's thoughts and feelings. That they were bound together. Maria felt reassured, that there was absolutely nothing to fear regarding the consequent physical separation from her family and friends. Somehow, she knew her loved ones would be all right, and that she need not worry for them.

"My dear Maria," Azrael said, "your spirit and energy will live on in Creation for eternity. While it is true that your terrestrial shell serves no further purpose for you, and will soon be as much dust, Creation has much need for your life's energy. As for your loved ones, theirs and your anxiety over your passing will be but a fleeting glimpse of sadness, for your soul was and will be forever bound to theirs in Existence. I wish the energy of every soul in existence could be as pure of heart as yours."

In a final effort, Maria pleaded with her mysterious visitor in an increasingly soft, though not entirely comprehensible voice, "Please…. Please linger a while longer…. just a bit." Azrael's presence was incredibly soothing.

His reply was warm and embraced every fiber of Maria's very core. "Uplift your heart. Prepare to cast off the delusions of this existence and welcome your awakening.[15] Allow me to cast a light into the furthest reaches of your doubt. Your existence is fulfillment. Exaltation and liberation presently await you!"

With those words, Azrael once again leaned over Maria's bedside. As if she knew what to do, Maria promptly laid back upon her pillow and, still not taking her eyes off of Azrael's figure for one instant, relaxed herself. Azrael gently rested the palm of his right hand upon her forehead, and his left on the center of her breast just above the heart. The final sensation her mortal frame felt was like that of a warm shower dripping down all over her body until eventually it was totally enveloped, followed by what could only be described as the sensation of a soft kiss. The weary traveler, upon reaching the last stop on a great and arduous journey, received a departing gift.[16]

"Welcome home."

✳ ✳ ✳ ✳ ✳ ✳ ✳ ✳ ✳

The clearing of the evening sky was like that of a new beginning being ushered in. A great peace descended upon the sleeping city. As the remaining darkness of the early morning was gradually chased away by the first rays of dawn, the very last of the lingering clouds in the firmament made their way off into the distance in great haste, unveiling the full glory of the illuminating crown of the dawn sun.

Through the partially shut shades the sun dazzled the room in which the terrestrial body of Maria presently lay in perfect serenity, revealing that the soul of which had thus begun its eternal return to the energy of Creation.

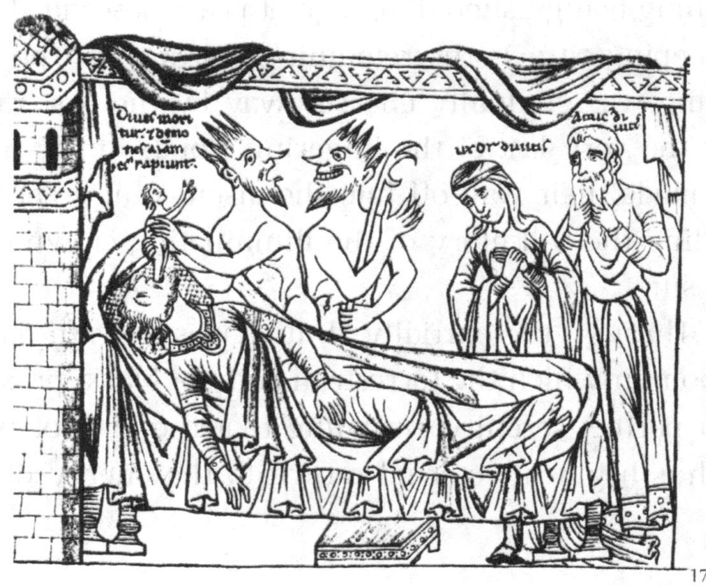
Diues mori
tur: ydemo
nes aiam
eius rapiunt.
uxor diuitis
Amic di
uitis

17

From house to house they dash along.
No door can shut them out,
No bolt can turn them back.
Through the door, like a snake, they glide,
Through the hinge, like the wind, they storm.
Tearing the wife from the embrace of the man,
Snatching the child from the knees of a man,
Driving the freedman from his family home.

Ancient Sumerian Text[18]

Chapter 4

Rays of increasingly brighter light began crawling little by little, inch by inch, across the still slightly damp cobblestone of this coastal city. Just a faint twinkle of daylight could be made out at the horizon, the glowing orb of the sun hesitating for the briefest of moments on its gradual ascent upward to begin yet another orbit around the planet. Almost as if pausing temporarily, the star seemed to stall to welcome the day prior to once again resuming its continued climb. Before too long, her magnificence would find its way into every exposed space, illuminating and invigorating every corner of Life of this space in time.

The town square quickly filled with every variety of merchants, or purveyors of goods and services, preparing, as is done every morning, their stalls in a tremendous haste for the flood of shoppers that would soon move through the numerous rows of the market. A short pudgy candlemaker greeted one of the local farmers in the adjacent stall with an obligatory hug, mingling for a few minutes over the latest gossip each was greedily eager to share. Otherwise, everyone was moving hurriedly about their usual routine preparations for the approaching day, enjoying the last remaining moments of peace and tranquility. Soon the market square would be crowded, shoulder to shoulder, with throngs of people all selfishly shoving about from stall to stall in a frantic frenzy.

Daybreak had traditionally been Azrael's single most favorite time of the day in the mortal realm. His spirit had often found, even if for only a glimpse, something so irresistibly pure and unvarnished in the nature of it. For Azrael, every morning that the countless numbers of stars graciously bathed and cleansed Creation, ushering in a rejuvenation of Life, was yet another reason to express his gratitude. Existence gestated because of, and with, every particle of light that passed continuously across the infinite expanses of the Cosmos.

While Azrael was pondering more existential matters, those mortals among whom he walked were variously preoccupied with other relatively unimportant thoughts and tasks. Walking about the market vendors while also watching the farmers and other merchants go about their arrangements in earnest brought a sudden flood of sadness. He thought to himself, *If only these terrestrial beings could comprehend even a small fraction of their limitless potential.*

Azrael observed person after person go about the errands for which those entities believed ignorantly to be of the utmost importance, intently searching each of their thoughts.

Do these creatures have any idea, or have they ever had even a fleeting question as to why Creation saw fit that they be organized into reality?, Azrael continued to ponder. *Why does it have to be at the instance of their passing before they finally come full circle with this understanding? These beings go about the time they have in this temporal realm pursuing such meaningless habits as though their terrestrial days are endless, eating excessively, desperately seeking worldly objects, carnal pleasures, and seeking after ever more wealth and power. The desires which mortals pursue are mere illusions; mirages they live their entire lives chasing that are in the end nothing more than dry beds of sand. False frivolities keep their cosmic energy from ever recognizing the true nature of Existence and their special connection with it. These terrestrial entities possess infinite access to energy, linked to Life itself and the divinity of Creation.*

After moving about the hustle of the market's many comers and goers for a period of time, Azrael eventually chose to settle himself at one of the tables of a small unassuming café adjacent to the square, not but a few steps from the commercial throng. Despite the scene of somewhat substantial commotion in the vicinity of the café, there were only a couple of tables occupied by customers. Azrael could not help but glance at the patrons of each of those tables. *Perhaps it is best that these people continue to exist completely unaware. They can, therefore, continue to go about their lives in perpetual simplicity, without ever feeling the weight or burden that such awareness would consequently bring upon them.*

He believed his choice of venue was entirely random, if not also devoid of meaning or significance. Time would eventually prove quite different. No being, mortal or otherwise, can escape Fate.

✳ ✳ ✳ ✳ ✳ ✳ ✳ ✳ ✳ ✳

While Azrael was thoroughly lost in his own thoughts, a young server from the café quietly approached him. Just as she was about to speak to him, she found herself overcome with shyness and feelings of apprehension, though she was unsure of precisely why. Once composed, the young woman broke the silence to ask, "Good morning, dear sir;

how may I serve you on this fine morning?"

Azrael did not immediately respond, or even acknowledge the presence of the young woman standing immediately beside him. He simply continued staring at nothing in particular, as if completely oblivious of her presence. The waitress instantly felt her anxiety increasing. Convincing herself that perhaps she had not been clear or loud enough, she attempted to speak again. "Dear sir, may..."

Before the young woman could finish repeating her question, though, Azrael turned ever so slowly to face her, causing her to choke on her words. Once their eyes met each other for the first time, they both felt a strange and unavoidable impulse to just stare at one another. Azrael sensed immediately the intense kindness of the figure next to him, while the young lady, for her part, was flooded with a mix of varying emotions; not least of which was the uncertainty as to precisely why she was feeling so excitable. Fear, apprehension, exaltation, relief, overwhelming joy, and anxiety were all somehow experienced all at once.

Sensing the young woman's conflicted emotions, it was Azrael who chose to initiate the conversation. "Please forgive me for being so rude. You caught me in a moment of distraction. I would love some coffee and a small pastry, if possible."

The waitress struggled initially to utter a reply but managed after a second to form a somewhat coherent phrase. "Ehhhh, yes, yes, I will promptly return with your coffee and pastry." In her extreme nervousness, the waitress turned quickly to escape and darted back inside the café. Azrael watched as this young lady stepped away from him. There was something about how she carried herself that betrayed a natural dignity that one does not traditionally find among others of her social condition. Her mannerisms and speech were common enough. The clothes she wore were expectedly tattered, likely patched together dozens of times. Nevertheless, Azrael paid no attention to such trivial things. He could sense a tremendous, glowing aura. A powerful energy radiated from this woman.

A few minutes passed before the server returned with Azrael's order. She gently placed the several dishes on the table for her guest, hands shaking a bit in the process, causing the dishes to rattle some. "Here is your order, good sir," was all she managed to say.

Azrael turned and looked deeply into her eyes for a few seconds. "Thank you. I'm sure that I will enjoy it." At the same time, he thought to himself just how profoundly beautiful this creature was, inside and out, but at that moment could not identify precisely why.

The woman standing before him possessed no immediately distinguishable qualities. Like nearly all young women of her terrestrial species, her skin was fair – almost glowingly so. Though pulled up and concealed within a bonnet, her hair was a brilliant platinum and shimmered ever so faintly when the sunlight caught it at just the right angle. Her features were at first glance meek, though, with time, they revealed a great deal of inner strength.

The young woman lingered for an embarrassingly long time before finally stepping away from her patron. She could not, however, help herself from looking back occasionally in quick jerks, staring at the stranger, curious as to who he might be, and what business he must be about. Something about his mannerisms and countenance drew her in, mesmerizing her completely. Several times she found herself desperately wanting to approach this man, to interrupt his breakfast and ask him the several questions circling through her mind. Eventually, the urge became far too uncontrollable and irresistible. She felt overwhelmingly compelled to know exactly who her mysterious guest was; though, she did not understand precisely what caused this compulsion.

With a tremendous courage entirely foreign to her, the young maiden pushed forward toward Azrael again. Once she reached the table at which he was sitting, she fully anticipated that she would freeze with apprehension. Nevertheless, and to her own surprise, she found that she was not apprehensive, but was in fact propelled with a renewed sense of vigor. She subsequently, and rather boldly, sat herself down in a chair across from him, facing him directly, almost shocked by her own fearlessness.

Neither spoke for what was probably only a few seconds, though for the young woman it felt like several minutes. Finding it difficult to not take careful notice of her guest's appearance, the waitress could see clearly how remarkably handsome he was – almost impossibly handsome, she admitted to herself. Other than his beauty, this man sitting across from her was arguably ordinary in every way, his physical features no different in nature to any of the young men in her community. He had a head of wavy, dirty-blond hair, and equally golden, radiant skin. Nevertheless, there was something powerfully unique about him.

This time, it was Azrael that interrupted the awkward silence with a boldness of his own. "May I ask your name, if I am not being overly forward?"

Stunned briefly, and not entirely expecting the question, the young waitress did not answer immediately, but rather adjusted herself awkwardly in the chair. Something about the nature of Azrael's general countenance, however, helped calm her nerves, and she felt comfortable for the first time answering him. "My name is Johanna."

Azrael lifted his cup of coffee and took a quick sip,

searching Johanna's eyes for a moment. "It is indeed a pleasure to make your acquaintance, Johanna. I am Azrael."

The two remained locked in each other's gazes. It was at this moment that Azrael realized how attractive Johanna truly was. Not a refined and bred beauty one occasionally finds, or expects to find, among the more well-off families within any given society, but a more humble, natural attractiveness. One that just peeks through the surface, hinting at what is underneath, but, given the chance, would sparkle like a well-polished pearl, outshining all others, if it could only escape through the silt of its clam shell. Johanna was likely completely unaware of just how comely she was, and perhaps that was what helped qualify her beauty.

A moment later, Johanna felt, with another surge of courage, intrepid enough to ask the one thing that had been lingering on her mind ever since the stranger initially sat down in her family's café. "May I ask who you are? Please forgive me. I know how out of line I am being, but, you see, you are clearly not from around here, are you? By that, I mean that I have not seen you before, and I am familiar with most of the families in this quarter of the city."

Johanna immediately regretted her line of inquiry, wishing desperately to retreat. Azrael simply smiled, though, and looked gently into her eyes, sensing her increasing anxiety and feelings of profound foolishness. His next words were carefully chosen and selected with the specific intention to satisfy her intense curiosity as much as to relax her mind. "Do not concern yourself with offending me. You may ask me anything you wish. To answer your question.... yes, you are correct – I am not a local."

"What brings you to our humble corner of the world then, if I am indeed not being too nosy?" asked Johanna, with some lingering apprehension. "Most outsiders we encounter are traders or merchants in search of something. You appear to be neither."

"And how can you tell that?" Azrael said, chuckling as he did.

"Your appearance gives you away. Your boots, sir, are not worn down to paper thin strips of leather as one would expect from years and long miles.," answered Johanna matter-of-factly.

Azrael was not sure how much he should divulge to this young lady. Besides the very obvious existential fact that he was forbidden to do so, he was quite certain that sharing the complete truth – or even a small fraction of it – would be cosmically catastrophic, not to mention that there was no chance that this simple creature could possibly grasp anything.[19] A mortal being could never fully grasp what they were told, to start with, of the nature of his role in the greater workings of Creation, let alone Eternity. What mortals did, or could, potentially and imperfectly render from what was presented to them would, Azrael had concluded many millennia before, only serve to utterly confuse, totally confound, and ultimately lead to the addition of more false spiritualism than already existed for these multitudes of easily misguided souls.

So, Azrael chose to mask the truth, while still providing a relatively believable answer for the sake of furthering the conversation. "I, am, in my own way, in search of something."

Johanna scrutinized Azrael's expression, and quickly concluded that he was intentionally avoiding any details, giving the briefest answer possible. The abnormal twitch of the lips and the sudden wrinkling of the brow were just a couple of obvious clues. Rather than push the issue, Johanna let it go. She allowed her facial muscles to form a partial grin, yet her expression betrayed that she knew he had not been completely forthright with her. Azrael, for his part, decided that it would do no harm if a stranger knew a little about why he was in her town, especially if such truth were sufficiently masked.

Looking down at his shirt to brush away a few crumbs of pastry that had accumulated there, Azrael replied, "You are right in believing that I was holding something back. I'm in fact in search of an estranged acquaintance. We have been separated for many years. As it turns out, my search for him has brought me here, to this small corner of the world."

Johanna, with the same sweet smile with which she had first greeted him, bid her strange customer the best of luck in his search. "I do hope you have the best of luck in finding your friend, and may your reunion be joyous. In the meantime, please enjoy your stay here. While this city does not have the many charms offered by other larger, and much more worldly cities, we are proud of her." Feeling as though she had prodded far too much with her mysterious guest already, Johanna decided it best to end the conversation.

Getting up to leave, Johanna paused once more to look back at her intriguing customer. Azrael gave his own salutations, sensing Johanna's intentions. "I too hope my visit proves to be advantageous. Perhaps we will cross paths again, Johanna. Until that time."

"Perhaps..." was all she managed to say, before skirting back nervously.

As Johanna hurried away, Azrael thought to himself, *I hope...though I fear it will not be so. I'm afraid this visit will not be pleasant at all.*

Chapter 5

"I am the bringer of the Light, I am of the Light, I am the Light.[20] I am the final companion and Eternity's twilight guide. I am Malak al-Mawt.[21] I am four thousand wings carried by the Winds of Time.[22] I am Thanatos.[23] I am the Harvester of Souls, the Autumn of Creation, and the Twilight of Time.[24] I am the bringer of everlasting comfort. I am fulfillment, transcendence, and liberation of Creation's never-ending cycle.[25] I am that which serves the boundless will of Existence. I am seventy thousand feet, and infinite eyes and tongues. I am Eternity's scribe. I am the Last. I am Azrael, the Angel of Death."

"For I was, in the very beginning, an everlasting resonance. Once a member of the Council of Light, the Seraphim Council, I was possessed with the Divine Authority of overseeing Existence as one of that body of Eternal Watchers.[26] Nevertheless, I was caught having committed a most grievous violation of the Law of Eternity.[27] My essence mingled with a being of flesh and found carnal companionship with the mortal creature – a most serious violation of my sacred office, and a most shameful betrayal of my sacred oath. It was ultimately determined by the Council that my punishment would be that I must first live out a life as a terrestrial being, a human, and therefore suffer and enjoy all that a mortal must, only to, in the end, be torn from that of which I had grown so fond. For the remainder of Eternity, I would then serve as the immortal guide to the beyond for the energies of the very mortals so very dear to me, to be constantly reminded for all time and space of the consequence of the affections I once incautiously chose to share.[28]

"As a corporeal being composed of imperfect flesh and blood, a carbon lifeform brought into reality by the Energy of Life, formed in the forge of Creation, I was, as such, veiled for a time from the greater truth of my previous circumstance, and was destined to perish back to the dust from which I arose.[29] As a mortal I was thus named Azra, he who is helped by God, the first-born son of Malekesh.[30] In terrestrial life I was nothing more than a humble physician, as my father before me, and his father before him. Though I certainly did not deserve it, I was blessed with a wonderful companion and three beautiful children. On all accounts the chains of my corporeal life could have been described as blissful. I try to not think about those beings long since departed, for it only stirs up stubborn feelings of longing that are best left dormant. For lingering memories of my terrestrial companion still weigh heavily upon my essence.

"While I never at any point believed that I had solved any of *life's* lessons, in my utter blindness I thought that I had a strong understanding of a few principles based on my people's traditional spiritual beliefs. As with all corporeal entities, I lived in an existence of absolute ignorance of the true nature of Existence. In many ways, and for many obvious reasons, I wish the circumstances of my mortal ignorance had remained thus.

"When my physical frame was no longer sufficiently suitable to act as a carbon vessel for Existential Energy, my spirit, as I once referred to it, was released from its terrestrial tethers. My essence was once again filled with Knowledge, the purest recognition of what I am, along with the disappointing memories of my betrayal of office. Disappointing not because I was ashamed for having allowed myself to love, but rather because such a construct was, and for eternity will never be, permitted to such as I. Therefore, I called back all of the parts of my essence that had once been shared with others in love.[31]

"Before there ever was, the carbon creatures that formed as the natural offspring of the Energy of Existence lived and died with no regard given by Existence for what came to pass from the energy that once animated those deceased beings. However, circumstances in Existence evolved the need for order and harmony in all of that expansive chaos. It was commanded that my essence serve Eternity by ensuring that the life forces of righteous and worthy creatures be returned safely to Creation, to provide for that continued balance of Celestial Order. Thus began the most current phase of my everlasting sentence.

"Mortal life began to be recorded in the Annals of Existence. The energy signatures of all beings are therefore listed for all time and space, or Ethereal Scrolls.[32] When Creation finally calls out across the Universe for the return of an essence of life, one of the blessed, one encircled in light[33], I, for my part, guide that essence to re-emerge once again with Existence.[34] The names of all mortal beings are recorded on the leaves of the Tree of Life, or more precisely, the Register of All Mankind.[35] When those leaves fall, I am there to gather them up unto me, and then collect the souls written upon them back to Creation.[36] I am present at the end, to be a guide and a comfort.[37] This is the sacred duty placed before me for infinite time and space. It is a task for which I am forever grateful, for it allows my continued existence to remain in constant contact with the physical realm, and thus what it means to be mortal.

"I have witnessed the collapse of immeasurable galaxies, seen the formation of countless planets and stars, and I have stood vigil over innumerable species of mortal beings. All of this for periods beyond comprehension. Is this a blessing or a curse – I can no longer tell.[38] Eternal rest, I seek, but may only find when the last of the living has passed the threshold into the beyond. Until that eventuality, I am bound in the service of Creation, never to enjoy an eternal slumber. My purpose is my sacrifice, and my sacrifice is my purpose."[39]

Chapter 6

Later in the day, just shy of the sun's descent below the amber horizon and the ushering in of yet another night, Azrael slowly made his way through a graveyard just on the outskirts of a quaint town, taking his time as he casually passed row after row of aged headstones. While he never at any point believed that he had solved any of *life's* lessons he noticed several people gathered around one of the nearby plots, just past a small outcrop of spruce trees. Besides himself, this gathering appeared to be the only collection of personages of any kind within immediate sight. Azrael gradually approached the small crowd, drawing forward to observe them much more closely and intimately, before ultimately stopping at the grove of trees that separated them. Being sure to use the relative density of the group of trees as cover so as not to be seen, Azrael peaked curiously across at the bereaved. There was a light evening breeze beginning to stir, blowing in his general direction, just enough to rattle a few of the leaves and allow the approach of a slight sound to reach him. Azrael could pick up on most of what would be said, if anything at all, by those somber figures off in the distance.

The small gathering around the freshly covered grave site appeared to be that of the loved ones of the individual that had very recently interred. Not one person standing beside the buried remains of the corpse, wearing their finest mourning garments, made a sound or movement. Rather, they just stood as reverently as possible, keeping silent vigil. The funeral services were long since over. Those grieving chose to remain for a few lingering moments, unwilling to pull themselves away. They found it difficult to step away, as if by doing so would in some way be showing disrespect to their deceased loved one. So, they just stood.

For those few in attendance, the death had been a particularly strange affair. The departed man had been just shy of sixty-seven years of age, and his health had been deteriorating recently. Family and friends alike had been preparing themselves for some time for the eventuality of his departure from the mortal realm and, when it came, it would have been without any discernible evidence of foul play, were it not for the look of abject horror on his corpse's face. It was impossible for them to know the truth of the tragic nature of his death - that his physical form and life force had been prematurely torn, quite violently, apart from each other. One might consider that a blessing.

Once again, Azrael recognized immediately that another life form for which he was solely responsible had been claimed, not by him of course, but by another essence which had yet to reveal itself. Azrael knew full well that he would have been tasked at the proper time to collect this righteous being, but only when the man's name appeared upon the Ledger of Eternity. He, and only he, was given the proper authority to reunite the souls of righteous creatures with Creation. If Azrael's suspicions proved to be accurate, and the cosmic essence referred to as Samael was in fact behind this rash of brutal and unsanctioned abductions of souls, there would be no telling what evil Samael planned to unleash.[40]

After the family and friends of the deceased had finally withdrawn from the scene, Azrael took a moment to walk around the discolored, freshly filled grave site, looking about him carefully. When he had been ordained with the eternal mission of ushering the energy of departing beings back into the fold of Creation, the Council had endowed him with the power to interpret the Ethereal Echo.

The Ethereal Echo, Azrael knew, would reveal everything he needed to know or understand about what had really happened to this formerly terrestrial being. From the very beginning, from the moment of Eternity's primordial origins, there has always existed a record of every corporeal entity that ever was, is, and ever will be. The Ethereal Echo is essentially the energy signature or disturbance left behind by the Life Force of those carbon-based creatures; like a quantum shadow imprinted in the Annals of Eternity. Every living terrestrial being, no matter its origin or condition, impacts the cosmic timeline, and Azrael can use that record in order to learn things that have transpired for which his essence was not an immediate witness. The Ethereal Echo eternally woven in Eternity provides those able to read it with the ability to understand what has and ultimately will transpire.

Unfortunately, however, there are only a few essences like Azrael with the cosmic power to challenge the fates of eternity, let alone outright defy them, and, therefore, rewrite the future entries in the Annals of Existence. While the Cosmic Fates are clearly fixed for mere mortals, there are a few eternal essences that have the Authority of the Universe bestowed upon them by Existence, and can, with such authority, challenge the storyline of Existence.

Azrael could not tap into the doings of this unholy scene without first engaging with, and seeking consultation from, beings possessing certain Celestial Forces adequate to the task. Calling upon the forms known by savage, mortal tongues as the Grigori and Mercurian, Azrael sought guidance in order to interpret precisely what was to be derived from the Ethereal Echo. Together the Grigori[41] and the Mercurian[42] have the authority to dissect the remaining threads of energy strung delicately between a mortal's decaying remains and the life force of their late existence, creating a Perception Roll which would essentially describe for Azrael the identity of the deceased, and finally unfold the nature of how this terrestrial being met its end.

With the assistance sought, Azrael began to investigate what remained of the Ethereal Echo and disturbances left behind on the Ethereal Record for clues as to precisely what had taken place, who was involved, and where the soul's Life Force had ultimately been taken. A very alarming and equally disturbing circumstance began to unfold, in the same way a sequence of vivid memories might play back in a mortal's mind. Every detail, each fraction of each moment, revealed itself to him as though not only were he a direct witness to the events in question, but had experienced them himself. As the scene unveiled itself, Azrael grew overwhelmed by feelings of utter despair. He recognized a sensation taking hold of him that he had never before felt – pure fear. Not fear necessarily of what was being revealed to him of how this fine creature had expired, but fear that he might not be able to accurately piece together any conclusive answers quickly enough to intervene.

For it was a scene in which the most hideous forms to have ever existed, the Keres, purposely sought out and savagely tore the soul of the dearly departed from his once healthy and vibrant mortal shell. The Keres are the vilest defilement of Existence, essences so disfigured and twisted by the wickedness that birthed them as to be unrecognizable as essences of Creation. These immortals of utter aversion feed on and lust after destruction, satiated by carnage.

The body of this poor mortal being lay gasping desperately as the Keres severed its life's energy from its terrestrial frame, ripping it apart in the process. These abominations fed ferociously as vultures might, desperately devouring a corpse as though it were their last meal. Azrael was filled with unspeakable anguish and agony at experiencing the screams of the deceased's soul as they reverberated madly across Existence. The deadly work of the Keres only took the smallest fraction of an instant, but the consequences were now everlasting. Azrael interpreted that the Keres had fled with the remains of the departed upon completion of their evil task. Yet no evidence whatsoever was observable, which only served to further frustrate him.

What was also painfully clear now, however, and despite the complete lack of answers, was that a cosmic essence with substantial authority was directly involved in the disturbances that had recently been perpetrated on the planes of mortality. The Keres were the awful servant creations of only one such essence – Samael. They were obedient to him only and did his bidding exclusively. If the Keres were involved in any way, then Samael would essentially be confirmed to be either directly or indirectly involved as well. Azrael knew instinctively that it was up to him to find out precisely what role Samael had played in the recent collection of cosmic disturbances and to what purpose was the ultimate end game. He felt a deep sense that he would not like the answers he sought for his queries and was even more disquieted by all of the un-pleasant potentialities swirling through his intelligence.

43

"And now I will tell you how he died. His days were sixty [years], when a sickness attacked him. And his days were not as the days of David his father, but they were twenty [years] shorter than his, because he was under the sway of women and worshiped idols. And the angel of death came and smote him [in] the foot, and he wept and said, "O Lord God of Israel, I am conquered by the terrestrial law, for there is no one free from blemish before Thee, O Lord, and there is no one righteous and wise before Thee, O Lord."

The Kebra Nagast, by E.A. Wallis Budge[44]

Chapter 7

When the soul of someone is determined by the Cosmic Record to be unworthy of being reunited once more with the Energy of the Universe upon its passing, the unholy creatures known as Keres are tasked with dispatching the soul in question. The Keres first ruthlessly ravage the mortal entity's spirit while violently separating the carbon vessel's Eternal connection with the Energy of Creation, before finally devouring the life energy so as to extinguish any ethereal remains of the tainted energy so that it cannot pollute that of Creation.

Keres were not always the foul demons into which they eventually evolved. For longer than is conceivable to attempt even a simple explanation, the essence known as

Samael, by order of the Cosmic Council, had been charged with the enviable responsibility of eliminating the souls and Life Energy of the unfavorable creations across Existence.[45] Samael allowed himself to be increasingly corrupted by the sheer power of his magnificent importance, becoming an essence that relished destruction and misery above all else. Samael had come to represent the counter-balance to Creation and Existence. It was Samael that first handled the passing of evil souls. Merely performing his cosmic responsibility was, however, not enough for the Angel of Destruction. Instead of eliminating all of these unrighteous creatures for which he was assigned by the Cosmic Record, Samael used the Cosmic Power bestowed upon him to twist and deform many of those beings into devilish monsters for the singular and despicable purpose of serving his every command. Rather than executing his cosmic function with the dignity that inherently accompanies a Cosmic Entity, Samael now embodied that which he was supposed to annihilate from Existence. He began using the Keres, the minions he forged from hate, to do his dirty work. They are the eternal slaves of evil, *the Tenebrae*, the approaching darkness.[46]

Keres are, therefore, nothing more than the mangled, defiled form of what was once the soul, or life force, of a terrestrial being. They sadly no longer have any resemblance to the life form that was once birthed by Existence into Creation. Rather, they appear more as demonic shapes out of some unthinkable nightmare. No one set of descriptions could possibly come close to properly characterizing the appearance of a Ker, for they are merely distorted, decaying forms of nothing any longer distinguishable, partially inhabiting a realm somehow between both mortal and ethereal planes at the same time. What is clear, however, is that these defilements constantly thirst for blood and Spirit, a never-ending desire that can never be sufficiently quenched.

The filthy work of these demons is, for the growing number of their victims, the single greatest instant of agony and suffering a creature of Existence can or will ever experience in a thousand iterations. While only for a fraction of a fraction of a moment, and ultimately ending in the elimination of all cosmic traces of the unfavorable soul, the experience unfortunately and irrevocably serves as the Universe's final judgment on the tortured creations.

For the passage of infinite time and across equally infinite space the Cosmic Council has allowed for Samael's grotesque eccentricities largely because he had always been an obedient and loyal servant, and his peculiarities had never resulted in any noticeable or egregious imbalance in the Universe. Azrael, for his own sake, while not appreciating or respecting the methods employed by Samael, never himself had any reason – until recent events

– for which to consider Samael a concern.

Azrael's suspicions were, nevertheless, increasingly leading him to the deplorable conclusion that Samael was in some way behind the recent incidents of not wicked spirits being cast out, but of innocent souls being prematurely eliminated. His fears were leading him to believe that Samael was not just involved but was in fact the perpetrator of this sinister affair. The problem faced by Azrael would be in uncovering the details of these abominable deeds and discovering Samael's ultimate end game. Samael's suspected actions were finally beginning to create a noticeable imbalance in the Universe, an artificial and unnatural asymmetry that would very quickly become eternally irreversible. Azrael pondered deeply the horrific idea that it was Samael's aim to create such an imbalance, and to use that imbalance in his favor for some despicable, and not yet discernible purpose. What was more terrifying for Azrael were all of the possible motivations Samael may have for increasing his power and ranks. Azrael was growing more aware that uncovering the apparent plot would be the easiest part of what was to come. Stopping Samael from achieving whatever his ill intended ambitions were could likely tear Existence asunder.

Chapter 8

The sun was just beginning to make its slow rise to once again illuminate its planetary companion for yet another daily terrestrial cycle. From Azrael's humble vantage point facing out onto this city square, the fresh beams of morning light from the sun began creeping up between the white sandstone of this city's beautiful baptismal building and the equally impressive co-joining cathedral. While Azrael had seen literally infinitesimal numbers of just such sunrises, he never grew tired of their magnificence. He cherished and bathed in that brilliance. Sunrises were a powerful and frequent reminder of just how thin the veil is that separates the Physical from the Ethereal planes.

It was in this precise moment of resting and casual

contemplation, while absorbing the rays of the new sun, that the young mortal woman, Johanna, with whom Azrael had only just recently become acquainted at the market café, nervously approached him. While he was fully aware that the young maiden was now standing only a few short paces away from him, he did not immediately choose to acknowledge her presence. Rather, Azrael gave pause.

Which is the brighter of the two objects before me: this glowing celestial orb or the radiant countenance of this beautiful woman? Azrael asked himself while still not yet making eye contact with Johanna. The humor behind this thought was not lost on him and, therefore, this private question had the effect of bringing a smile to his face – a rare moment.

"Good morning, Johanna," Azrael said, seemingly catching Johanna a little off guard. She herself was lost in the moment, perfectly comfortable with allowing her strange new acquaintance to continue sitting looking off in silence because that provided her with the opportunity to merely continue to stare at him, whilst losing herself in his eyes. It was now Johanna's turn to ignore him.

When she was finally ready to respond a few moments later, she answered, "Indeed! It is a fine morning, good sir. Quite splendid."

Azrael once again grinned, though, this time the smile that formed on his face was caused by the overly formal manner with which Johanna insisted on addressing him. "And where would a fine young woman such as yourself be headed on such a blessed morning as this?" he continued with equal formality, despite knowing full well the answer to his question.

Was this man mad? Johanna thought to herself. *Did he not clearly know which day of the week it was? Even if he did not, could he not also see the throngs of people shuffling their way across the cobbled square to the adjoining cathedral?* Despite being genuinely confused by the figure standing before her, Johanna did not utter her questions aloud, believing them to be relatively inconsequential. Rather, she replied, "Good sir, I am on my way to join the rest of the community at the first mass this morning. Were you planning to attend?"

First turning to face the direction of the massive open doors of the cathedral, Azrael observed the growing crowd of parishioners making their way inside for the mass to which Johanna referred. He then looked back to face Johanna, though he did not respond immediately. Instead, he sought to choose his words judiciously first. "I have already communed sufficiently with Divinity this day."

Upon seeing the disappointment come across Johanna's face in the form of a growing frown, however, he quickly added, "Nevertheless, one may never have nearly enough spiritual contemplation? Yes. I too will soon make my way to the chapel."

Instantaneously, Johanna's frown was replaced by the most brilliant smile of almost uncontrollable, raw enthusiasm. Sometimes Azrael almost forgot just how seriously many corporeal creatures considered the matters of their institutions of faith and spirituality. It was and is a characteristic unique to mankind – one of several peculiarities that set them apart from nearly all other such creations of Existence.

And, why not? There was certainly no harm in spending what would have been a dull and lonely morning in communal reflection among these beings within the walls of the ornate building they hold to be of spiritual importance. Azrael quickly came to the conclusion that any reason he had for ignoring Johanna's courageous invitation was purely selfish. Afterall, he was, at that very minute, seeking temporary respite himself from the troubles for which he had been engaged. And having been mortal himself once, he had often found such peaceful places as this to be helpful in seeking serenity, no matter how momentary it may have been. There was always something so comforting about the dull echo reverberating off of the marble columns and walls during collective prayer, the sweet smell of incense lingering in the air, and the gentle kaleidoscopic glow of the light cast through the numerous stained-glass windows.

With tremendous apprehension, Johanna dared to ask, "Wou…would you honor my family by joining my parents and I in the congregation?"

The invitation touched Azrael deeply. "Your family honors me with such a considerate invitation. A request I find impossible to refuse. I graciously accept."

The smile that had touched Azrael's heart moments before returned immediately to shine from the gentle contours of Johanna's face, arguably brighter than before. He promptly stood, whilst returning the smile. Almost simultaneously the two turned to face and began moving toward the now well-illuminated cathedral. They walked a pace apart the whole way in an oddly comfortable silence. Each instinctively knew that no further words between them were necessary.

✶✶✶✶✶✶✶✶✶

Anyone observing the morning devotional ceremonies on this particular day would have witnessed a tremendous crowd, relatively speaking, of faithful in attendance, all quite prepared to demonstrate their fealty and steadfastness. One would also be forgiven for not being able to identify the stranger from amongst this dense gathering, for his form was simply lost in the mix. Azrael, for his part, was perfectly satisfied to go unnoticed, or at least to not have anyone make any serious inquiries into the nature of his association with either Johanna and or her family. His responsibilities required the utmost discretion and anonymity. He was fully aware of the great risks he was running in openly engaging with mortals as brazenly and frequently as he was. It was of course a fine line; however, he was willing to tread it if only to feel and experience what it is like to walk among mankind again, and to embrace their beautiful ignorance.

The beginning of services was completely overlooked by the visitor, who was already lost in contemplation. One might even describe his state as one of deep meditation. Perhaps it was a response to his current location, or because of the being next to which he was sitting, or both. Whatever the case, Azrael was rather powerless to cast out certain stirrings and sensations that were swirling around within.

These terrestrial carbon realities, of which Azrael had once counted himself, are so blindly intent to follow, and dogmatically obey, these mortal institutions promoting supposed principles of spirituality and salvation from some perceived pre-conditions of existence. This strange obsession with trying desperately to understand and interpret the meaning of their lives through the imperfect lens of religiosity ultimately only leads them down a path of further confusion. Azrael wished he could reveal some truths to these creatures, if only to set their cloudy minds at ease in order to relieve some of the existential burden they undoubtedly carry. Nevertheless, he knew with assurance that terrestrial life, no matter where and when across Existence, did not have the capacity for properly processing any other potential reality, whether true or not. The truth would only serve to further confound their undeveloped intelligence.

Corporal beings, essentially, exist because they can exist, and for no other reason than that the Energy of all Creation begets Life; energy conceives matter. Existence of the Cosmos is because it is, and for no other reason.[47] The Energy of Life exists because it has always permeated Existence, and for no other explanation. Just as a balance between the positive and negative forces of the Energy of Life, there is also a balance between creation and destruction in Existence. The positive Energy of Life, which binds while at the same time coursing through Existence, is wanting to constantly create Life. The negative Energy of Life seeks the destruction of that which is created, and, therefore, counterbalances the forces of Existence. The intelligence and energy known as Azrael has, for nearly an eternity, helped maintain this fine balance of Existence.

Mortal creatures accomplish absolutely nothing by binding themselves to these notions of salvation and obedience to a perceived deity or deities. The only noticeable byproduct that Azrael has ever observed has been the perpetuation of hate, distrust, malice, and disunity between beings, often resulting in a distortion of the Energy giving life to these imperfect forms. Ultimately, and unfortunately, this leads to disharmony across Existence for which Azrael must continually work harder to re-balance. But this is Azrael's infinite duty.

Chapter 9

When the simple worship service had finally reached a conclusion, the parishioners all began to make their way slowly out of the cathedral in a steady succession, stepping back out into the square to be greeted by the full brilliance of the sun. The air was beginning to warm quickly, chasing away the lingering morning chill. As each of them entered the sun's light, they took a moment to appreciate its warmth before reverently continuing about their day - a somber day of rest for most.

Azrael was careful not to stand too close to Johanna, for he knew instinctively that others of her kind would be more observant of those around them now that their attention was not immediately focused on something else.

Azrael was well aware of the strict cultural norms prevalent among groups of mortal creatures of this place and time. He followed a few steps behind Johanna and her parents as they made their way into the square, pausing when he noticed them pausing. Johanna leaned in close to her parents and appeared to say something brief that he could not quite catch. Then she embraced, and kissed, both her mother and father, before turning to face him.

Johanna's father glanced in his direction, the person with whom his only child, and, therefore, only daughter, had suddenly chosen to spend her time with. Azrael could not distinguish precisely what her father saw, but whatever it was did not, apparently, concern him, for he ultimately gave a quick approving nod, and softened his eyes.

Johanna said her goodbyes, then moved over to rejoin her new friend and together they watched her parents shuffle away. Both her mother and father occasionally looked back over their shoulders as they did so, as was only to be expected of curious and concerned parents.

"The weather today is quite spectacular," Johanna said. "I intend to take a walk. I sincerely hope I am not being over-presumptuous but wondered perhaps if.... well..."

That was all she could get out before she was seized with nervousness – an anxiety that she was being too forward with this person she hardly knew, and a person of the opposite gender at that.

Looking gently back into Johanna's eyes, Azrael could read everything he needed to. Not from this sweet woman's words of course, but from her countenance and soul, which expressed everything she could not utter aloud. Her feelings were obvious and clear, like the dancing flames of a bonfire on a dark, moonless night.

Azrael's response immediately put her at ease. "It would be a privilege to join you for a walk. A walk is just what I need to calm my mood. Perhaps it will give me time to ponder some things with greater clarity. I only hope that you will not tire of my presence or feel obligated to keep me company out of some notion of hospitality."

Johanna could not hold back a chuckle at the dry sarcasm she sensed. "I often venture out for a stroll after services beyond the East Gate just outside of the city walls. It is so peaceful, and the view of the city from the hillside is perfectly marvelous."

Azrael simply smiled and nodded gently in approval, and the two began walking off in the direction of the sun, still climbing toward its zenith.

✶✶✶✶✶✶✶✶✶✶

Very little was exchanged between the two over the course of their walk beyond this little speck of civilization. Perhaps this was due in part to some lingering nervousness for Johanna, or perhaps because both Johanna and her male companion intuitively understood that sometimes words are entirely unnecessary. All that needed to be communicated was exchanged sufficiently each time their eyes connected in subtle glances.

When the silence was not enough, though, it was Johanna who would venture the occasional question. "When we first met, you mentioned that you had come to this insignificant part of the world in search of someone. Have you made any progress in finding whom you seek?"

Azrael immediately stopped walking. Johanna's and Azrael's eyes met. She noticed a sudden shift in his countenance from one that had been relatively relaxed, to one that was now obviously sad and disturbed. She instantaneously regretted her line of inquiry and made an attempt to apologize for seemingly upsetting her new friend.

"Please forgive me!" she nearly shouted. "I'm a foolish girl sometimes, and do not always know my place. Forget I ever asked such an intruding thing," Johanna added with a spasm, beginning to come to tears and turning away as she did so.

Azrael quickly recognized that his sudden change in mood had effectively and unnecessarily startled this young woman and therefore, immediately interjected, softening his facial expression at the same time. "Dear Johanna, you have said nothing for which you should be ashamed or embarrassed, and certainly have nothing for which to apologize."

While not knowing precisely how to calm Johanna's nerves, Azrael did perceive that he needed to make sure this young woman was put at ease. He then slowly stepped forward to face her and, lifting his right hand to her cheeks, he softly brushed away the tears that had begun to trickle down her face. This, and Azrael's words of assurance, had the intended effect of bringing the sparkle back into Johanna's eyes. Giving in a little to temptation, he allowed his hand to linger at Johanna's cheek for a bit before retracting it to his side once again.

"I am, as it turns out, having a rather difficult time tracking down the individual that I need to find. My task has proven insurmountably more challenging than I had first expected. Your question simply reminded me of that unfortunate reality. That is all. It is I that should apologize to you for startling you so. I should have been much more measured in my response," said Azrael.

"You must think that I am a silly girl for getting so emotional," Johanna replied with a bit of a whimper.

Shaking his head emphatically, Azrael indicated his disagreement, and added, "On the contrary!"

Azrael now faced a decision that he hoped he could have avoided while appearing as a mortal being. That decision inevitably being whether or not he would reveal himself to someone of the terrestrial realm. Of course, the irony of his circumstance was not lost on him, for the only one to blame for having become so intimate with a mortal to begin with was himself. The difficult and awkward situation in which he found himself was entirely of his own making. He knew the tremendous risks and, despite those risks, chose foolishly, nonetheless, to take the chance to experience mortal intimacy once again. He just had to decide how open he was willing to risk being. After quick deliberation, Azrael chose rather to be judicious about what he revealed to Johanna, and consequently decided that it would be unfair for an immortal essence such as himself to unload such a burden upon a terrestrial entity which would effectively lead to complete bafflement and likely terror.

Continuing, Azrael stated, "My troubles need not worry you. Let's not allow this to ruin such a wonderful outing."

Johanna shook her head in agreement, and the two began walking again.

Though his last words were filled with optimism and encouragement, Azrael was not sure if he meant them more to reassure Johanna, or to convince himself. Either way, they were disingenuous.

The pair walked on for some time more, enjoying sporadic conversation before they both came to the unfortunate realization that the sun was beginning to make its inevitable descent beyond the reaches of the horizon. The mutual, yet unpleasant, decision was made to turn back. While deep down the two knew it was an eventuality both expected, they both secretly hoped that, somehow, despite the immutable Laws of the Universe, the sun would in some way defy those principles by which it was eternally bound, and linger a period longer in the firmament, allowing for a sliver of more time. Of course, this could not happen, and Azrael therefore walked Johanna back to the simple home in which she lived with her parents.

Upon reaching the front door, he graciously thanked his companion for the pleasant time. "I enjoyed our time together tremendously. Being in your company, and the walk, was precisely what I needed. It is unfortunate that we must say our goodbyes."

Gazing affectionately back at Azrael, Johanna replied, "I agree completely. Perhaps we will have an occasion to meet again soon." And before Azrael could follow her by saying anything else, Johanna rapidly lunged forward and placed a quick, yet sweet, kiss on Azrael's right cheek. Then, and just as abruptly, Johanna opened the front door to her parents' home and retreated inside, closing it behind her.

Completely overcome by emotion, Azrael just stood outside Johanna's home for several minutes. Part of his essence was overjoyed by the feelings coursing through him. The other part, however, realized the utter absurdity of it all. Absurdity because no matter how much he longed for the mortal experiences he had once enjoyed, cherished, and thoroughly missed, he was playing with fire. Azrael recognized the sad truth that eventually he would end up breaking Johanna's heart – something that devastated him to admit.

✷✷✷✷✷✷✷✷✷

Meandering very slowly, almost at a crawl, and feeling quite foolish as well, Azrael wandered about the city, lost in thought. It was during this episode of reflection and introspection that he suddenly had the strong sense of the stirring of unpleasant spirits about. He instantly stopped, remaining absolutely motionless.

Observing the space and time between the mortal and immortal planes, Azrael caught the approach of a large host of Keres moving on the Stellar Winds in the direction of the setting star. There was no time to lose. Azrael knew instinctively that this may literally be his only chance at beginning to get some real answers. He immediately made haste to investigate where and what the Keres were up to.

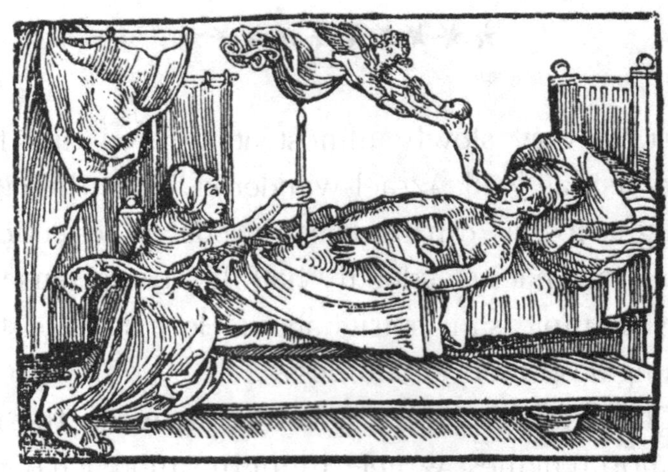

48

"Then Allah said to the second of the three angels, '"Go thou, and fetch a handful of Earth's dust."' He, too, flew swiftly down to Earth and tried to gather up a handful of its dust, but when he saw how the Earth shook and shuddered, and when he heard its groans, the gentle angel could not do the deed but let that which he had gathered fall, dust unto dust, and lifting up himself, he returned ashamed and weeping to the Presence of Him Who had sent him. And Allah said, '"This task was not for thee. I blame thee not, but stand thou too aside, and other service shall be thine."' Then Allah sent the third angel, who descended swiftly, and gathered up the dust. But when the Earth began to groan and shudder in great pain and fearful anguish, the sad angel said, "This sore task was given me by Allah, and His Will must be done, even though hearts break with pain and sorrow."' Then he returned and presented the handful of Earth's dust at Allah's throne. And Allah said, '"As thou the deed hast done, so now the office shall be thine, O Azrael, to gather up for me the souls of men and women when their time has come; the souls of saints and sinners, of beggars and of princes, of the old or young, whate'er befall; and even though friends weep, and hearts of loved ones ache with sorrow and with anguish, when bereft of those they love."' So, Azrael became the messenger of Death."

Folklore of the Holy Land, Moslem, Christian and Jew, by J.E. Hanauer[49]

Chapter 10

Azrael pursued the despicable Keres quickly yet made sure to not give away any indication that he was following. It was vital that he catch the demon spawn just before they acted upon whatever dastardly commands they were instructed to fulfill, so as to have the exact proof and evidence he needed of the evil unfolding throughout Existence. If the Keres were to sense that anything at all was amiss, they would assuredly flee, and he would undoubtedly lose any chance of ever getting to the bottom of this threat before it was too late.

The Keres glided upon the Cosmic Wind, being carried effortlessly along. As cosmic essences it took virtually no time at all for the Keres to finally reach their destination in time and space. And for Azrael, it was but a brief

quantum instant before Azrael noticed the obvious intentions of these fiendish creatures. They had arrived at a
humble farmhouse of an unimportant rural community
and began immediately to encircle the home as a swarm
of hellish locusts might, intent on devouring.

For what was less than a nanosecond in mortal terms, Azrael pondered precisely what his next move
should be. He fully recognized that this was the moment
of no return, that his actions from this point forward
would apply irreversible ripples of consequence in both
time and of space. What was also equally undeniable was
the truth that there was no absolute certainty that the
outcome or outcomes of his decisions would end with Existence recovering its proper balance. On the contrary, he
had to accept the unpleasant reality that the Fates of the
Universe were no longer set in a motion recognizable to
him, but, rather, were now to be rewritten anew and if he
were unsuccessful in ending this growing menace across
the Universe, Existence could, and likely would, collapse
into the utter darkness of Chaos for eternity.

His initial impulse was to immediately intervene
and put a stop to the evil with which these beings were
about to commence. Yet, he found himself pausing, questioning his very instincts. The full awareness of the gravity of what the chain of eventualities he was about to put
into motion surfaced, and that gave him a momentary re-

luctance to act. Despite that temporary lapse, Azrael gathered his composure sufficiently, and jumped into the fray.

The Keres were now gathering in and about the singular bed chambers of this simple farmhouse of an unknown mortal of absolutely no renown or importance whatsoever. They were about to engage in the vilest of acts upon that creature when Azrael allowed his presence in the very same room to be perceived by the Keres. The demons immediately froze cold and cocked their mutilated forms to face Azrael, maintaining a fixed gaze upon the intruder. While the Keres were indeed initially startled at being discovered, they were agitated more than anything else. As with other forms of creatures of prey found on the terrestrial plane, Azrael sensed the Keres begin to grow tense in anticipation of his imminent attack and agitated for a fight. He steeled himself for what was about to begin.

At the precise moment that the horde of Keres, as an entire disgusting swarm of hideous deformations, lunged toward him, Azrael stretched forth his arms before them, and summoned the cosmic authority with which he was ordained. With only a thought, he caused the very fabric of time and space to fold in on itself, and thus locked the Keres into the Quantum Void – the nothingness between the mortal and ethereal realities. The particles of Energy giving these vile essences their virtual animations were now essentially stuck in the chasm between all potential actualities. With an interstellar shockwave, Azrael pronounced, "By the authority of Everlasting Judgment laid upon me by the Cosmic Council, I do pass sentence upon you!"

Before passing final judgment, Azrael knew that he first must squeeze out as much information from these Keres as he possibly could. Otherwise, his having intervened in this matter would be meaningless. He therefore seized the life force of a single Ker. While slowly splitting its energy in two, Azrael ordered the Ker to divulge everything. "What cosmic essence is responsible for commanding you to annihilate the souls of the innocent? I demand answers!"

Despite fully expecting the response to confirm his growing suspicions, Azrael was, nonetheless, still utterly stunned by what the Ker, garbled and distorted, uttered back. "AaagghSamaaaaellgggrrraagghhh!" the Ker let out in a chilling shriek. With some difficulty, Azrael made out the name Samael.

Azrael had to take a quick moment to gather himself before continuing with the interrogation. He followed by asking, "To what dastardly end does Samael have the Keres perform these shameful abominations?"

In an equally horrifying sound the Ker replied, "Aaaghhhrrrbuuidddldzzrrghhhaanhhhrrrggarmyzzzrr-rgg!" As before, Azrael struggled to understand what the

Ker was expressing to him. He was, however, able to make out enough. "Build an army."

Azrael snapped back, "What do you mean, *build an army?*"

In a terrible and sadistic gurgle, the Ker began what Azrael could only make out to be a laugh, then followed by replying, "Hhhhggggrrrr.... seeeizerrrrggzzzeeexisttenc-cegggaaahrrggg!"

Despite an even greater struggle to comprehend the Ker this time, Azrael deciphered just what he needed. "Seize existence."

With an apparent effort to frustrate and at the same time intimidate Azrael, the Ker added, "aaagggzrrrhnorrr-rzzggaaaahhgmatterzzzrraaahgg...allrrrggghhhaaiszzzzrr-rggghaafallenggggrrrrhhhaaa!" ("No matter, all is fallen!"), followed by more sinister laughter. This time, though, the Ker's unsettling laughter did not cease.

Enough had been divulged by this point for Azrael to piece together what the Ker was inferring. And now that this remaining Ker was no longer of any value to his investigation, Azrael moved quickly to dispose of it. In the time it takes a particle of light to cross the Universe and back, Azrael ripped the Ker's life force asunder, leaving not a trace of its former reality in the spectra of Existence.

Eliminating the Keres, however, did not have the effect Azrael hoped for. In reality, it brought absolutely no comfort whatsoever. And unfortunately, he knew the inci-dent would ultimately prove meaningless. Disposing of the Keres solved nothing and, Azrael had to admit to himself, might arguably have made matters more challenging in the long run. How much more aggressive would Samael become as a result of his actions and obvious involvement in trying to stop his machinations was a question he did not want to have to ponder.

The other question weighing heavily on him was exactly how he was to bring an end to Samael and his destructive schemes. Eliminating a group of Keres was one thing but dealing with Samael would be something com-pletely different. He too was ordained with the Power of Judgment, as Azrael had been. The other unknown variable that needed to be considered was how much more pow-erful Samael may have become over the course of enact-ing his despicable plans. Azrael worried that, ultimately, he may be doomed to fail, unless he were able to enlist the help of other cosmic essences.

The encounter with the Keres, while obviously unpleasant, and something for which Azrael genuinely wished he could have avoided altogether, did prove valu-able in the sense that it gave him a wider peek behind the shroud of absolute mystery surrounding Samael's in-tentions. While several things were still entirely unclear to Azrael, there was one thing he knew with regrettable surety. The eternal being known as Samael was and had been attempting something horrendous, something evil on a scale never before conceivable.

Thus far, all of the evidence gathered and witnessed forced Azrael to make several unfortunate conclusions. His interpretation of what the Ker had uttered was that Samael was in the process of gathering an army unto his cause. That cause, as it seemed, was to manufacture an imbalance between the realities of Existence, and ultimately destroy it. In order to accomplish this, Samael had commanded his demon spawn to unjustly remove the Energy of Life from righteous beings, and, therefore, use that power to strengthen the negative reality of Existence. Hence, the imbalance of the Universe.

Existence would, if Samael's unholy works were not countered, spiral into nothingness; the complete absence of all that was, is, or ever would be. Would the Seraphim Council step in to support his efforts against Samael and, if so, would it be too late?[50] Only the Fates would eventually tell. One thing was certain – Azrael knew he had to at least bring these matters before the Seraphim Council and seek its guidance and wisdom.

Chapter 11

Traveling by way of the Cosmic Winds, along the Ethereal Plane, Azrael's essence found itself before the Seraphim Council instantaneously. It was in this same energetic form which he would also communicate with this divine congregation – one energy signature amongst others. Azrael was completely unsure of whether or not his report would be received with the full sense of urgency deserving of it. He suddenly understood, for the first time, that Existence, as it was, is, and would be, rested squarely upon his essence.

The Seraphim Council welcomed their beloved servant,

Azrael, as it always had, and in the unified response, "*Az-rael, loyal instrument of Existence, what need have you of this body?*"

After first hesitating, Azrael reluctantly began, "Eternal gratitude, Great Ones, for allowing me this audience. I bring an urgent report of what I have reason to believe may be evil tidings."

"*Please, continue; speak freely,*" the Seraphim Council echoed, inviting Azrael to continue.

"Forever bound to travel time and space on behalf of Existence, and in the fulfillment as such of my divine calling I have been witness to and privy of a growing body of evidence that leads me to believe that a cosmic essence, one very close to this Great Council itself, has been acting with the purpose of ultimately disturbing the fundamental balance that exists between the forces of Good and Evil," Azrael's essence began.

There was no initial response from the Seraphim Council, so, therefore, Azrael took this as a sign that he should continue with his remarks. "Across the vast expanse of the Universe, there have been righteous souls whose Essence of Life have been ripped from them prematurely by Keres, the demon creatures that do Samael's bidding. Thus, those souls are ultimately being consumed by the Negative reality rather than that of the Positive. For this reason, it must be assumed that Samael is involved in some way with these actions that are clearly intended to cause the harmonious balance that maintains Existence to gradually and inevitably unravel. Unfortunately, I do not know anything more with certainty at this moment. Nevertheless, I felt strongly that this had to be urgently brought before the Council."

There was once again no immediate reply. Azrael was thus beginning to grow concerned when the Council finally uttered, "*Dearest Azrael, faithful and eternally loyal servant. Gratitude. You speak the truth. We have also taken notice of the unpleasant stirrings of which you speak. Up to this point, we knew not what was becoming of so many un-reclaimed souls. Your presence before us now, nevertheless, confirms the dire nature of this matter. We urge you, Azrael, to continue looking into these unfolding conditions, and return in haste with further report. We will, meanwhile, ponder upon these concerns.*"

Azrael suddenly felt a measure of calm course through his essence, not because the matter of Samael and what he may be involved in had been resolved to any small degree merely by this dialogue, but rather because he hoped that this was a sign that he was no longer alone in dealing with these coming challenges that would surely be faced. Azrael felt some confidence, though not entirely so.

Before exiting from the divine presence of the Seraphim Council, Azrael paused to take stock. *My mission is now very clear.* Then he returned to perform his calling on the physical plane and resume his ongoing investigation of the unfolding evil throughout the Universe.

Chapter 12

Even before the beginning, there existed two opposing forces in perfect balanced harmony, one countering the other in a seamless flowing equilibrium of dual realities. Those dual realities eventually birthed equally opposing energies, the Positive and Negative actualities. These polarized energies then gave seed to matter bearing either Positive or Negative life forces – the offspring and eventuality of Existence. And thus, were wrought Good and Bad in the parlance of carbon lifeforms. There cannot be one without the other. Despite the never-ending obsession that terrestrial creatures have to constantly strive desperately to eliminate all things that are deemed *evil* from their corporeality, what they completely fail to grasp is that the nature of their very materiality can only be because of the counterbalance of the Negative. This absolutely necessary eternal stasis in the polarization of the Energy of Existence has now been threatened, nevertheless.

There was, however, a fraction of time and space during which one fundamentally important existential circumstance was not quite understood about Existence. When mortal beings passed away it was not guaranteed that their respective energies would be reunited with that of Creation. In some cases, it was so, while in others, the *spirits* of carbon creatures remained in a sort of cosmic limbo, destined to be stuck for Eternity in the void between quantum realities, the chasm between the ethereal plane and their formerly physical one, in Oblivion. There was not a cosmic mechanism for ensuring an essence's smooth transition from a terrestrial life form back to its original source. This threatened condition had the effect of creating an imbalance between positive and negative forces within Existence. This was primordial chaos.

When the carbon shells created by either one of these forces can no longer sustain the cosmic energy contained therein, that portion of the Energy of Life must be cycled back into Existence in order to continue and maintain the crucial harmonic flow of the opposing energies of Life ultimately begetting new creation. It is an eternal cycle lacking a beginning and or end. Existence only is because there has been an ongoing tranquility between the realities within Creation. Any partial tip of the Cosmic Scale toward imbalance would result in Existence collapsing in on itself into nothingness. That nothingness, or absence of Existence, would become the only reality of Eternity. Nothingness would beget nothingness. Out of necessity, Existence allowed for cosmic essences, endowed with an infinitesimally small fraction of the source of the Energy of Creation, to serve to maintain the continued symmetry upon which Existence is predicated. The Seraphim Council thus oversees all possible eventualities and inevitabilities to this end. It is this very same divine council that subsequently began to notice that the essences of mortal souls were going missing.[51]

Various aspects of some phenomena of the Cosmos were still not completely understood. Some of the essences within the Seraphim Council believed strongly that the spirits of some beings were reincarnating, while still others might be getting stuck in Oblivion perhaps. Nevertheless, these were merely theories that needed to be investigated.[52]

The Seraphim Council, for its part, set apart several expedients in order to assist with the efficiencies of maintaining order in Existence, ordaining those essences with the Word of Death, and, therefore, the proper authority to carry out their celestial callings.[53] In order that the negative and positive powers of Creation recycle properly, the Seraphim Council determined that there was sufficient wisdom in endowing essences responsible for overseeing these two opposing realities as they retire from the mortal creature that they ushered into being and returned to the Origins of Existence.[54] It was additionally decided by the Seraphim Council that the essences most suitable for these respective responsibilities should be formerly corporeal creatures, their previous mortal condition providing an invaluable perspective in the roles they would be assuming. Azrael and Samael were the two formerly mortal beings chosen.

Azrael and Samael were once mortal beings. Azrael's terrestrial experience was the second iteration of his energy, no different from the other carbon creatures of countless numbers brought about by the Energy of Existence. They would, by all definitions, have been described as wholesome persons, men that garnered a tremendous amount of respect by others of their carbon-based kind. Among their respective peers, or those that knew them, it could even be said that Azrael and Samael were the wisest among them; men sought out for council and guidance. Of all the organisms of Creation, the Seraphim Council found wisdom in selecting Azrael and Samael from amongst infinite Creation. Thus, the entities once known to mortality as Azrael and Samael were set apart with a particle of that

Source of Existence, referred to as the Word of Death. With this sacred authority, Azrael was tasked with escorting the life force of positive creations, while Samael, for his part, with those of the negative. Together, therefore, an eternal balance was established and has been sustained for time immemorial.

For millennia upon millennia Azrael has faithfully served Existence and the Seraphim Council to remove dream-shades, otherwise commonly referred to by mortals as ghosts, from their tether to the corporeal plane. On occasion he brings comfort to departing souls, spreading a doctrine of peace and tranquility. This is in direct contrast with the role of Samael, and the category of terrestrial creatures for which he is responsible. For Samael would have the souls in his charge fear their final moments of recollection, terrified of the fate that awaited them. Both Azrael and Samael are, however, forbidden from being directly involved in the natural course of a mortal's existence, including opposing or counteracting any wrongful actions of other celestial essences. By decree of the Seraphim Council, in adherence with the Laws of Existence for which they are obliged to uphold, angels of death may not have a hand in causing or preventing a mortal being's demise. How a corporeal entity meets its end is not up to an angel of death but is rather entirely up to Fate and Fate alone, just as random as the formation of terrestrial life is out of the Energy of Creation.[55]

With the Word of Death, Azrael and Samael have the ability to exist in and move freely between the Ethereal, Oblivion, and Physical planes of Existence.[56] This dual nature is absolutely critical, allowing for authority in all dimensions of Existence. Azrael and Samael have always maintained the sacrosanct balance in Creation, and the Laws of Existence have, consequently, always been obeyed strictly...until now.[57] Something has clearly changed for Samael. A terrifying plot is beginning to unfold before Azrael.

58

"When it came to pass that Moses was about to die, Samael, the angel who is filled with enmity towards man, came before the throne of the Most Holy One and said, "Give me permission to take his soul from Moses." But God said to that angel who is named Severity of God, "How wouldst thou take his soul? From his face? How couldest thou approach the face that looked upon My face? From his hands?"

The Confounding of the Angel of Death, pg. 55[59]

Chapter 13

"I am the destroyer of Life.[60] I am the bringer of Evil, enmity toward all Creation.[61] I am the Accuser, and the chief amongst Satans.[62] I am Dumah[63], the adversary of mortal creatures.[64] I am Mashhit, and the Angel of Tuesday; the ruler of Fifth Heaven, Machon, and of the First Hour.[65] I am a poison and a plague upon Creation.[66] I am the severe wrath of Existence. I am Chaos unchecked. I am the Last. I am Samael, the Angel of Death."

✹✹✹✹✹✹✹✹✹✹

"In a time and place, long since passed and long since forgotten, I was. A brave and great warrior was I among my kind, celebrated for my tremendous prowess and abilities on and off of the battlefield. There were none amongst my people who were my superior. Many valiant, distinguished, and worthy combatants fell by my hands whilst I took breath. For this reason, the mortal beings of my race chose me above all others to be their figurehead of unquestioned authority. Guided by a firm fist, singular and unwavering focus, and swift retribution, my people were governed into an age of unparalleled prosperity and prominence among other terrestrial creatures. The tranquility of my reign would not, however, last. Subversive and dishonorable elements plotted and moved through my people like a cancer or virus, spreading falsehood and corruption. In the end, Creation called me home well before it was my time.

"Instead of ultimately reuniting with the source of the Energy of Life to begin my everlasting rest, a reward deserving of all notable warriors, my essence was constrained to serve Existence's bidding, and as such imprisoned for eternity. For infinite time and space, I have tirelessly gathered the most despicable among essences of deceased carbon entities, the damned, those encircled by darkness, forced to confront my own premature demise forever, while facing the reality that my own peace will never come to fruition.[67] Existence writes the names of mortal beings on the leaves of the Tree of Life. When those leaves shrivel and scatter and fall, I gather them, and col-lect the souls written upon them for final elimination.

"I will be infinitely resentful of my fate. As stated in the colloquialism of the physical being I once was, the last laugh will be mine. Before I am done, Existence will cease to be, thus bringing about my final rest. It disturbs me not that the termination of my essence also coincides with the same outcome for Existence.

"I am tired."

Chapter 14

After a significant period, according to the common means of measurement in the physical realm, Azrael finally took a moment to contemplate over and digest what he had unfortunately uncovered, and to attempt to formulate a much firmer notion as to what Samael was plotting.

What I now know, and the evidence of which I am now aware, must be shared immediately before the Seraphim Council. Haste is crucial, Azrael thought to himself whilst lingering in Oblivion between the Ethereal and Physical planes. Without any further hesitation, he once again made way for an audience with that great body.

Once in the esteemed presence of the body of the Seraphim Council, Azrael was welcomed and embraced once more. *"Welcome, faithful one. What have you to report?"*

"With the help of your servants, the Grigori and the Mercurian, and blessed with their capabilities to interpret the Ethereal Scroll, we were thus able to accurately trace and unmask what has become of so many lost souls. These souls in question, the essences of these formerly righteous mortal beings, are being reconstituted as evil spirits, and released upon the Terrestrial Plane to further serve Samael's machinations," Azrael began without worrying over formalities or frivolities.

"Continue," the Seraphim Council, as one, commanded.

Azrael proceeded without delay. "It is clear to us now that Samael is not only directly involved in this evil, but is the very entity behind the plot, guiding and nurturing the evil. Samael has been directing his servants of damnation, the Keres, to seek out and devour the essences of good mortal creatures and return to him with the energy of those former beings. In turn, and despite the prohibition to do so, Samael is using his cosmic powers to reincarnate some of these essences in carbon form as negative spirits, while the others are condemned to help him further widen the imbalance growing in Existence. Additionally, evil souls that should have been terminated back are being tethered to the corporeal plane as dream-shades and commanded by Samael and directed to influence and encourage evil among the living. I believe strongly that it is Samael's intention – to bring about the collapse of Existence into Nothingness. The precise reason, the nature of his motivations, or why Samael has turned away from Existence remains an absolute mystery. As your humble servant, I seek out the Council's divine guidance and leadership."[68]

"*This Council is indeed greatly disturbed by these recent revelations,*" was all that the Seraphim Council said, with a relatively lengthy pause, even by the standards of eternal essences.

Azrael waited in awkward anticipation, and when the Seraphim Council finally continued, their tone was serious and filled with tremendous solemnity. "*These are grave and terrible tidings you bring before this Council and require responses equally as grave and unfortunate. Because of his dastardly intentions, the results of which, if left unchecked, will prove to be eternally catastrophic, Samael has unmistakably set in motion circumstances and conditions that will ultimately threaten the sanctity of the cosmic balance, and with certainty will eventually tear apart Existence, unless he can be stopped, and his actions be reversed.*"

Once again, the Great Council was silent, and once

again, Azrael found himself awaiting further communication.

Finally, the Seraphim Council continued, "*Azrael, loyal Son of Existence, Right Hand of Creation, your essence never chose this cosmic assignment, yet you are fulfilling your calling with the greatest dignity and honor that any essence could. With boundless sorrow we hesitate in asking of you what we deem we must.*"

Before the Council could finish, Azrael interjected. "Ask it of me, I beg; whatever be the sacred will and desire of the Great Council in its divine and limitless wisdom."

"*But, Azrael, you already know what this Council requires of you,*" proclaimed the Council.

And it was true. Azrael already understood the significant responsibility that lay before him. It was his burden to bear to find a way not only to put an end to Samael and his Keres from any further cosmic acts of evil, but then to reverse the imbalance already created by their actions. The most troubling question still remaining, however, was not whether he had sufficient determination to carry out this new calling placed before him, but whether or not he could do enough in time.

The Seraphim Council went on, "*The task for which you are now required is of absolute necessity for the continuation of the vital harmony of Existence to be restored. Of all the essences of the Universe, yours has al-*

ready proven its worth across Creation beyond measure. Your humility and singular dedication of purpose honor Existence. This Council wishes it did not have to call upon you to deal with this monumental matter, but as you yourself have already recognized, you are only one of two essences endowed with the Word of Death. Even this Council was not set apart with such magnificent power. Therefore, only you have the proper authority to stand up to your counterpart, Samael.

"This Council will not, however, release you to deal with Samael without also placing an advantage before you. The Laws of Existence prevent thee from exercising the necessary command to deal with this particular challenge. Nevertheless, Azrael, Eternal Flame of Hope, we, the Seraphim Council, Eternal Overseers of Existence, does hereby bestow upon your essence the Power of Judgement, and as such raise you in status above that of Archangel, with prominence over the essence Samael, and providence over the necessary galactic resources. Additionally, we have ordered our Mercurian and Grigori to accompany you on this dangerous mission. Hence, with this new ordination, and the Cosmic Power therewith, you and your Servitors will have the appropriate authority and blessings of Existence to restore balance back to it by whatever means necessary."

Azrael allowed the gravity and significance of the

reverent proceedings to sink in deeply before returning a response. "I am what I am – the humble offspring of Creation. Ultimately, I am what Eternity requires me to be."

With that, Azrael instantly departed the presence of the Divine Council.

✲✲✲✲✲✲✲✲✲

Azrael reflected deeply on the conference with the Divine Council, the commitment he had made, and all of the implications arising as a result. He was forced, therefore, to accept the bitter and harsh realization that, while he was confident that he understood relatively well the schemes of Samael, and despite having brought this to the attention of the Great Seraphim Council, he was essentially and admittedly no closer to stopping Samael's evil plans. He was likewise forced to admit to himself that uncovering Samael's intrigues had not actually accomplished anything consequential, just as meeting with the Council had equally little overall or immediate effect. The stark reality was that without a forthright plan for countering ongoing developments, Azrael was doomed for utter and hopeless failure, and thus Existence too would simply collapse into nothingness and cease to be.

To simply state that Azrael was contemplating the next steps he should take in moving forward would be the single most gross misstatement. He was utterly racked and tormented with trying to calculate and recalculate the most plausible pathway forward to effectively counteracting Samael's ill intentions. The more elaborate the ideas were, however, the more convinced he became of how spectacularly they would likely fail. The knowledge that giving up was in no way a consideration only exacerbated the mounting pressure that lay upon his essence.

How can I possibly help Creation meet Samael's evil?!, Azrael eventually asked himself in tremendous frustration and anguish. The question seemed innocent enough, though, it was one that likely had no probable answer, or likelihood of generating any useful results. Azrael almost posed it to himself rhetorically, believing full well that it would bear no probable fruit. It was, nevertheless, in this relatively simple question that, quite remarkably, the spark of the answer for which he was seeking began to slowly emerge.

Could it actually work?, Azrael pondered.

Azrael thus surmised that the most productive course of action would be to use his enemy's own tactics against him. He would, therefore, direct the Grigori[69] and Mercurian to stop and eliminate the Keres and retrieve the souls lost to the Negative, while he, Azrael, Agent of Existence, would gather the Energy of Creation from unrighteous mortals on behalf of the Positive.[70] Once Samael was neutralized, Azrael could detain him, and bring him for trial before the Seraphim Council, which would hand down a fate worthy of his evil deeds.

Despite understanding instinctively that his plans for counteracting Samael were quite obviously fraught with difficulties, twists, and unforeseen hurdles he was too naive to yet comprehend, Azrael knew it was the only idea that could logically withstand the challenges out-stretched before him. It was the one, and only, chance that Existence had, so he knew he had to make it work.

Chapter 15

"Gather unto me all of my faithful servants!" called Samael, whilst lingering in the Quantum Void between the planes of Existence. "The time has finally arrived and is indeed ripe for us to fulfill my destiny! Existence shall be no more, upon the arrival of the dawn of Darkness!"

As this message was being shared, a multitude of hosts of Samael's hideous Keres, along with equal numbers of the Life Forces of the innumerable kidnapped souls, as well as an assortment of other dark entities approached his essence and began to swarm around his presence like a cloud of locusts or some other such mortal plague. The scene would have been, if it were not for its catastrophic reality, quite tremendous in scope, the culmination of millennia of deceitful and backhanded scheming. Samael appeared to grow increasingly pleased with himself the longer he basked in the attention of the hordes of evil forms, his essence nearly bursting with an unholy exuberance.

Samael continued addressing the increasingly calamitous throng. "Greetings, my beloved children!" He then chuckled to himself as he perceived the sick irony in the statement. "Bask in my glory. Feed and draw everlasting strength from me, for I am everlasting damnation!" When Samael had paused, the multitude collected themselves before him, seeming to recognize instinctively that it was time to receive further instruction.

"My offspring, you have indeed been very laborious. This is a most pleasing thing to me." He chuckled again at this as he went on, "I can feel the very fabric of Existence beginning to tear and split along the seams of Reality. A surge of the Chaos is beginning to seep into those cracks that we have created together. I am supremely confident that, very soon, all that will implode, thus fulfilling our calling.

"The hour for which we have all awaited, the moment for us to push forward with the full magnitude of our strength, is nigh. No more hiding in the shadows and corners of Existence. Now heed my command. Go forth – ye are free to introduce as much mayhem as you desire.

Nothing shall stop you. From this point in time and space, there will be no way for any essence of Existence to conceivably unbind and reverse the path upon which we have set the Universe. The momentum is entirely ours. Go – let us finish what we have started, bringing about the end of Reality and, therefore, eternal suffering."

✶ ✶ ✶ ✶ ✶ ✶ ✶ ✶ ✶ ✶

As the countless number of savage essences that call Samael their master began moving off across the infinite expanses of Existence, Samael began pondering to himself, *The only looming uncertainties are how much of my designs Azrael is aware of or suspects, and whether he was successful in gathering the full weight and support from that unholy Seraphim Council.*

Azrael always was and will forever remain nothing more than a blindly faithful disciple of that twisted and demagogic body that claims falsely to act as proxy on behalf of Existence. The Council punishes his weakness as an immortal essence, finding him guilty of an unforgivable betrayal of his cosmic authority, and yet it subsequently rewards him with the privilege of ushering the righteous beings' essence's back to the source of all creation. I was, however, an admired and revered mortal being, never having transgressed. Nevertheless, I was instead placed

126

into eternal slavery of the worst energies to ever develop out of Creation. It would have been better that I had been erased from Existence all together.

Irrespective of what he may know, he could prove to be difficult in the end if he decides to act promptly to counteract my intentions. There is no possible way I can stand up against Azrael directly, especially if he is aided by the Council. If what has been reported to me by the Keres is true, then Azrael has found yet another mortal distraction. It is supremely disappointing that I cannot use the knowledge of Azrael's cavorting with the wretched corporeal beings with the Council, to remove him as an obstacle in my path once and for all. The tragic irony of doing so, however, would be that his downfall would be mine as well. This information, though, could prove to be useful in other ways.

I will, therefore, need to move ever more swiftly and cruelly if I am to successfully set in motion that which can never be undone. The full fury of my legions of minions must be unleashed across time and space, holding nothing back. And I know precisely how to begin. There would thus be no chance for any being, regardless of their authority, to counteract the sheer havoc that will be introduced throughout Existence. Azrael, and or any other slave of the Council, will find that they are utterly and thoroughly overwhelmed. For darkness will rush forth, consuming all *in its way. Only I will be left before Creation... left to snuff out the last remaining flame of Existence.*

71

"Presently the Death Angel met a devout man, of whom Almighty Allah had accepted, and saluted him. He returned the salute, and the Angel said to him, "O pious man, I have a need of thee which must be kept secret." "Tell it in my ear," quoteth the devotee, and quoteth the other, "I am the Angel of Death." Replied the man: "Welcome to thee! And praise be Allah for thy coming! I am aweary of awaiting thine arrival, for indeed long hath been thine absence from the lover which longeth for thee." Said the Angel, "If thou have any business, make an end of it," but the other answered, saying, "There is nothing so urgent to me as the meeting with my Lord, to whom be honor and glory!" And the Angel said, "How wouldst thou fain have me take thy soul? I am bidden to take it as thou willest and choosest." He replied, "Tarry till I make the ablution and pray, and when I prostrate myself, then take my soul while my body is on the ground." Quoteth the Angel, "Verily, my Lord (be He extolled and exalted!) commanded me not to take thy soul but with thy consent and as thou shouldest wish, so I will do thy will." Then the devout man made the minor ablution and prayed, and the Angel of Death took his soul in the act of prostration and Almighty Allah transported it to the place of mercy and acceptance and forgiveness."

'The Angel of Death with the Proud and Devout Man' (a tale from *Arabian Nights*)[72]

Chapter 16

The sheer and undefinable immensity of Existence is something that the means of utterance available to mortal creatures is simply too inadequate to comprehend and, therefore, explain. Many terrestrial beings across the vast reaches of Creation have often tried describing what they believe of the Cosmos. Nevertheless, their grossly imperfect sounds fall well short of the futile task. Perhaps that is precisely the point. No carbon-based entity, no matter how wise or enlightened they may be, could ever gather the right collection of syllables together in just the precise sequence to form the words that could allow them to ultimately and accurately portray the incomprehensible expansiveness of Existence, for the same reason that fallible beings cannot fully grasp the mathematical concept of infinity. Existence did not see it fit that temporal entities should be bestowed with such authority of understanding.

In the vulgar speech of many a mortal tongue, however, there is very little, if anything, that can be comprehended of the magnificence of Creation. Any attempted explanation of Reality, before even being conjured, would be wrong. Existence is truly infinite in the most exacting and literal definitions of the concept. Nonetheless, even that is a largely imperfect descriptor. Creation is not restricted, it is not limited, and it is forever expanding across boundless planes and dimensions. Creation is Existence and Existence is Creation, without beginning or conclusion, always Reality. All of what makes up the infinite breadth of Creation across time and space is both fragmented and in the same way one. The Energy of Life binds the very fabric of Reality, pulsating, entwining, and enjoining Existence.

This reality, this existence, was now being threatened with being unraveled by the twisted intentions of Samael.

✸✸✸✸✸✸✸✸✸

After leaving the presence of the Seraphim Council, and after the instantaneous journey within and across the vastness of time and space, Azrael had returned to adopt his

previous physical form among his beloved terrestrial carbon forms.

Upon the arrival of dawn, Azrael found himself facing and staring directly toward the scattering of the first
rays of daylight.

"I never tire of catching the magnificence of the
virgin light of day, the first waves of that invigorating,
luminescent energy, the very Energy of Life itself, bathing
everything in its radiance," Azrael whispered to himself.
"Were it that all creatures could or would appreciate it
so, for its purity. The Energy of Life discriminates against
none, reaching and blessing all." For a number of moments
more he indulged himself, admiring the gradual way in
which the daylight overtook the landscape around him
in small increments. He merely stood, arms outstretched,
chest and face lifted to the sky, waiting patiently for the
eventual solar embrace.

Azrael then began to take stock of the fact that Samael and his horrendous agents of devilry had begun what
could only be described as an all-out onslaught on Existence; a concerted push toward achieving an irreversible
imbalance thereof. Trillions, if not hundreds of trillions, of
innocent and righteous mortals were being smitten down
prematurely in some grotesque way with the help of Samael's minions. Unfortunately, evil was rising up to fill the
vacuum left behind in the wake.

Azrael thought to himself, *Clearly it is the intention of Samael to take action against Existence, before the Seraphim Council, or I, can initiate a response, or counterattack in some way. Was he aware of my suspicions, I wonder?*

Almost as soon as these thoughts had formed, a most intense and terrible fear quickly arose within him, ultimately seizing full control. *What of Johanna?*

Making all haste possible whilst inhabiting the physical form of a mortal, Azrael made the residence of Johanna and her parents. He forced himself to stop for a moment, however, as he came within a couple of dozen yards of the humble dwelling and attempted to bring his emotions under some measure of control. Azrael feared the horrendous possibilities of what he would find.

Resuming his approach, Azrael walked gingerly, almost exaggeratedly so. He took in his surroundings, observing and absorbing every detail. There was not a single sound; nothing audible to either mortals or immortals alike. Azrael was well aware of how ominous a sign that was. He strained his senses for some hint of life within the dwelling and found none. A chill washed over his mortal body. He uttered a silent prayer that he was wrong, that they were simply out. But deep down he knew he was too late.

Azrael concentrated on the inside of Johanna's chambers. Lifeless eyes stared up at him, that beautiful face pale and twisted in the scream of her final moments, all trace of her sweet, pure soul utterly destroyed.

He dropped to his knees, the mortal body he inhabited gasping violently, seized by excruciating anguish. What followed next cannot be fully understood or adequately explained in any language of even the most sophisticated of imperfect temporal creatures. The agony he felt, the pain of the knowledge he had failed her. Azrael took her cold hands in his and a scream tore from him, a cry of such a terrible nature as has never before and never since escaped any known entity or essence in Existence. "Ahhhhhhhhhhhhhhhhhhhhhhhhhhhhhhhhhhhh!!!!"

Azrael's cries rumbled and wailed from someplace deep within, reaching through the eternities and back out again with a thunderous explosion that shook the very fabric of time and space itself.

"What have I done?" A flood of tears ran down the cheeks of his mortal frame. "I am the author of this nightmare! Dear Johanna, my darling Johanna, please forgive my arrogance and foolhardiness. If it were not for me, your light would continue to shine upon this world for the continued blessing of those around you."

The feelings of utter guilt and anguish now flowed freely, like an unceasing torrent. Deep and profound regret gripped him. If only he had not surrendered himself to his feelings for this beautiful soul. Samael would have had no reason to select her, among the multitude of others, for destruction. In a manner of speaking, he had essentially placed the target on her back.

"Once again, my proclivities prove to be my downfall, and now the downfall of the one I adored as well." Anger seized him, and with great vigor, he vowed, "This ends now! This will be the last step Samael takes toward completing his evil desires. I swear it!" Still holding Johanna's lifeless hand in his, he stared long and hard at the face now in eternal slumber, and added, "Johanna, I swear on thy memory! You will have your revenge."

Azrael then leaned down slowly and placed a kiss upon the fading crimson of his beloved's lips. He allowed his lips to linger a moment, locked with Johanna's, secretly hoping that, when he drew back, she would be gazing longingly up at him, as if nothing had ever occurred. Alas, it was not to be.

Chapter 17

In light of the extremely harsh realities stretched out before him, Azrael was forced to stare into the abyss of truth and recognize that the initial plans he had made to halt Samael's machinations were naïve at best. "I was foolish to have been so simple-minded regarding my ideas for counteracting this fiend. It is painfully clear now that in order to stop and reverse the momentum begun by Samael, I will need to meet his actions with an equally bold response.

"There were certain measures that I was heretofore understandably unwilling or reluctant to undertake, certain countermeasures that are strictly forbidden by me under the Laws of Existence. Samael does not expect it of me, nor would the Seraphim Council for that matter sanction such blasphemous actions. He is counting on our strict adherence and obedience to these sacrosanct laws. Therefore, what he does not expect, he will also not suspect or be prepared for.

"I will use the sacred authority bestowed upon my essence by the grace of the Seraphim Council, along with the help of the Grigori and Mercurian, to set about the very thing of which Samael is not anticipating of me. In order to immediately begin the process of reversing all of the unsanctioned murders of all of those helpless lifeforms, taken without just or proper authority, the Grigori and Mercurian will be enlisted to restore those former entities with their Energy of Life, once again."

Azrael's plan, while perhaps relatively simple in the approach thereof, was, however, quite bold and audacious in its overall scope and breadth. Nevertheless, he knew with absolute certainty that that was exactly what was required in this precise moment. The time for such action had perhaps already, unfortunately, come and gone.

With the Grigori and Mercurian, Azrael would, one-by-one, resurrect as many of the prematurely deceased mortal souls as possible, and as quickly as possible, within the constraints and binds of Time and Space.[73] Traditionally, Azrael would not have been sustained with the authority of office to sanction or perform such resurrections regardless of the justification. The Seraphim Council had, however, found wisdom, given the dire circumstances faced by Existence itself, to allow him to exercise the Power Cosmic, and with said authority pursue whatever actions were necessary to stop Samael once and for all.

"I cannot allow myself to dwell on how uncomfortable it is to take actions beyond the normal range of my powers. These are only temporary measures for the greater good of Existence, and nothing more," Azrael tried to convince himself.

Azrael and his faithful Servitors would vigilantly seek out Samael's devilish agents and destroy them without mercy to the last remaining essence if necessary. Thereby ensuring that they cannot rise again to take part in such evil ever again.

Chapter 18

Convincing enough cosmic essences of Samael's dastardly intentions was going to be simple, relatively speaking. It was well understood that Azrael had the blessing of the Divine Council, and the support of that sacred body carried tremendous weight with it. That would be enough for some to heed his call to action. Not all of the immortal hosts across the Cosmos would be so readily convinced to take action, however. For some, Azrael's new authority would not be enough. Multitudes certainly recognized what must ultimately be done to stop Samael's evil plan. Unfortunately, getting those essences to align themselves ideologically with Azrael would not be a straightforward proposition, and would not even be the most challenging hurdle to cross. On the contrary, drawing enough heavenly essences that would be willing to dive into the abyss with him, risking their very eternal existence for the cause, no matter how justified and righteous it may be, might ultimately be the more arduous part of his mission.

Azrael set out as quickly as quantumly possible to recruit his army of righteous warriors for the unenviable quest of overcoming Samael and his menacing devils. As he suspected, it did not require much prodding to make other entities aware of Samael's eventual plans for Existence. Unfortunately, just as mortal creatures are not all inherently endowed with a sufficient measure of bravery, so too do eternal essences differ in levels of courage. While he would have desired, and even expected on some level, to have had many more beings answer the call to arms on behalf of Good, Azrael was grateful for the level of support he did eventually muster, and fully recognized that the war to come would not be won or lost based on their sheer numbers alone. There was more in play than that. His Servitors were a hardy collection among the essences of Existence, and they, Azrael was confident, would prove in the end to be formidable opponents to Samael.

One of Azrael's newly appointed Servitors, with great expedience, brought to the attention of the hosts of righteousness that Samael, at that very place in space-time, was already gathered with his horde of Evil. They were finally prepared, it seemed, to push forward with their intentions to finish what they had unfortunately begun.

The time had inevitably arrived. The dreaded moment was upon the forces for Cosmic Balance. They would be, in the space of time less than that of the transfer of energy from one atom to another, fully engaged in the hideous work of eliminating the opposing multitudes. Eternal essences far too vast to number using any known form of calculation would be wiped clean from the Annals of Existence in the coming cosmic conflict, realities from both sides of this eternal divide. The impossible scale of expected calamity was not lost on any being.

Azrael entreated those essences that had pledged support to do whatever was within the Cosmic Power available to each of them to stop the imbalance from tipping irreversibly. It was made painfully clear that in order to bring back a cosmic equilibrium, the forces of darkness must be eliminated at all costs.

"There is not a single essence that doubts the resolve of Azrael, but perhaps he does not fully appreciate the very precarious position he is asking us to take," interjected a large contingent of essences.

It was painfully true. Azrael had not thought of the

difficulties the varying multitudes would have in joining his cause. He had simply expected them to join him in the conflict to come. He had not taken the time to view circumstances from any other perspective or concern himself with any other reality other than his own. His focus had been single-minded, and reasonably self-serving. If he were going to have the slightest chance of building a coalition of not just willing combatants of the Heavens, but soldiers dedicated with the last measure of their very life force, then Azrael now recognized that he would need to address the very real apprehension of those gathered. The consequences of violating an Eternal Mandate were clear – Eternity in a state of perpetual ethereal limbo, neither existing nor not existing, in the void known as Chaos.

"You speak the truth," Azrael humbly conceded. "I was foolish to assume so much, and I beg forgiveness for my presumptuousness."

"It is clear to all in Existence of the severity of the circumstances faced by the Universe. None that are here now would be so if they were not committed to the preservation of the Cosmos. Nevertheless, the power we possess collectively is simply insufficient to do what we are being asked to do. Azrael may have been bestowed with special dispensation, with authority beyond his calling, but what of us?" the gathering asked. "This body risks eternal punishment by the Great Council for violating the Eternal

Mandates of our offices."

Before replying, Azrael internalized what was expressed to him. It was important to him that the sentiment shared was respected and valued. This was no simple errand he was asking them to embark on. He was asking them to potentially lay down their very existence. "Your dedication to and valiance for Existence is commendable. And you are all justified to be cautious. This is a very tumultuous time in space."

Azrael gave pause before addressing the throng once more. Even in mortality, he was never a being of eloquent words or flowery speech. He did recognize, however, that something needed to be expressed and transmitted that could not only help alleviate the understandable concerns of those essences present but would also stir the deepest passions within them to choose to join the fight despite those concerns.

"It has always been, is, and will be eternally so!" The energy behind Azrael's voice pulsed across the vast expanse of the Cosmos, reaching all. "The Energy of Life, which binds all, must be preserved with all means necessary by those that are willing to uphold the Balance. Concern yourselves not with the judgment of the Divine Council, for I, Azrael, will be your advocate before It. The Council set me apart for this unfortunate cause, and you are being asked to serve under my banner. I will champion your defense and assume the full weight and respon-sibility of any and all judgment that may come to you for overstepping Cosmic Authority. As essences of Existence, of what value are we to Eternity if, in this fractious moment of crisis, we, the offspring of the Cosmos, ultimately do nothing? Life needs us now more than any other moment in time-space. Existence requires us to take a tremendous leap of faith. Otherwise...." Azrael hesitated a moment in order to gather his final thoughts, "...this will all cease to have been, be, or ever be. Make thine stand with me!!"

Azrael's words had the effect for which they were intended. The instantaneous response he felt was that of an equally strong current or signature from the multitude of Heaven's realities in favor of support. There were not as many as hoped for, but Azrael had his army of the hosts of the Cosmos. "We are your servants until the end!"

The war for Existence had truly begun.

74

146

The Appointment in Samarra

The speaker is Death

There was a merchant in Bagdad who sent his servant to market to buy provisions and in a little while the servant came back, white and trembling, and said, Master, just now when I was in the marketplace I was jostled by a woman in the crowd and when I turned, I saw it was Death that jostled me. She looked at me and made a threatening gesture, now, lend me your horse, and I will ride away from this city and avoid my fate. I will go to Samarra, and there, Death will not find me. The merchant lent him his horse, and the servant mounted it, and he dug his spurs in its flanks and as fast as the horse could gallop, he went. Then the merchant went down to the marketplace, and he saw me standing in the crowd and he came to me and said, why did you make a threating gesture to my servant when you saw him this morning? That was not a threatening gesture, I said, it was only a start of surprise. I was astonished to see him in Bagdad, for I had an appointment with him tonight in Samarra.[75]

Retold by W. Somerset Maugham

Chapter 19

Azrael, carrying the full weight of the mission ahead of his armies, stood before his troops in anticipation of the coming struggle. Not only was he committed to being the first into the fray, but he was willing to be the first to suffer the ultimate end. The battalions of his Servitors and other allies were steeled for battle, not looking forward to it, but not about to back down from it either.

Gradually, and rather faintly at first, a sinister hum began to grow ever more distinguishable, emanating from points all across the Cosmos – a sign that the Keres were about to begin their onslaught. An indescribably terrible collective scream rang out. They had arrived.

As was to be expected, the fiendish forces of Samael were not going to simply step aside. Rather, Samael was emboldened, and the multitudes of the wicked were even more encouraged toward achieving the annihilation of Existence. Tragically, Azrael's forces did not escape loss. Fatalities among the regiments of light were regrettably heavy, cut down after being overwhelmed by masses of Keres feasting on their life forces. Despite early setbacks, Azrael's troops rallied. The tide of war slowly turned in their favor while they inflicted their own crippling justice. Using the newly acquired cosmic authority, the legions of Servitors seized upon Keres, and proceeded to extinguish their life force. The forces of Good and Evil locked in battle, engaging in ferocious and unthinkable carnage. They withstood wave after wave of the forces of darkness in pitched battle.

The spectacular and unimaginable energy bursts generated by the clashing armies were a shocking sight to behold. The tremendous intensity of the explosions of stellar energy nearly resulted in the collapse of the veil between the ethereal and physical planes. In the mortal realm, entire galaxies erupted, as hundreds of thousands of solar systems were consumed by violent blasts of radiation, leaving portions of the Universe uninhabitable.

Samael admittedly underestimated the resistance he and his followers would face from Azrael and were, therefore, unprepared to meet the initial challenge they posed.

Realizing that his armies were losing ground, he resort-
ed to unfathomable means in order to shift the balance
once again in his favor. Mayhem and wanton destruction
of life was left across the Universe in their wake. Samael had hitherto refrained from seeking out and attacking
immortal essences for fear of arousing a response from
the Seraphim Council before his plans had come to fruition. Instead, he chose to focus on mortal creatures. Azrael's intervention made it clear, however, that his intentions
were no longer unknown. Samael, therefore, cast aside all
remaining nuances of restraint and began a campaign of
total and merciless war against any and all, mortal or immortal, that he considered his enemy. Even ethereal essences not drawn into the fight were made targets.

The unrestricted onslaught against the essences of
the ethereal realm proved to be precisely what Samael
and his forces needed to turn the tides of the war in their
favor. The Keres, under Samael, regrouped and were emboldened. Large numbers of innocent realities were am-
bushed by the regiments of evil. Keres were essentially
given a free hand. Existence was burning in an infinite
number of infernos.

Azrael recognized that the war between good and
evil would inevitably become much more challenging
and equally calamitous to Existence before it ever even
began to inch toward improving. Unfortunately for him,

expecting the worst possible outcome did not help him or those fighting on behalf of righteousness, to digest the reality of experiencing it. They still had to face the stark harshness of the situation, no matter how brutally ugly and often terrible it became.

Samael mounted a formidable counterattack, which proved to be immensely brutal and devastating in scope. The life force of innumerable essences was lost, permanently wiped from Creation when their life forces were devoured by the Keres. The more energy the armies of darkness consumed; the further Existence tipped to the breaking point of imbalance.

Witnessing the devastation across the Universe had a disheartening effect on those essences remaining. More than a few of the Servitors felt their resolve pushed to the point of breaking, finding it nearly impossible to foresee the war ending in their favor, but not one faltered. And, if the stakes for which they had dedicated their very existence had not been staggering enough, those that wavered may even have been forgiven for their momentary lapses of conviction. Nevertheless, and despite having every conceivable reason to do so, Azrael and his Servitors never allowed doubt to divide or overcome them. No matter how grim and utterly disheartening the ultimate prospects may have seemed at times, Azrael and his Servitors never wavered. In the end, they remained absolutely steadfast and even bolstered in their resolve.

The counterattack of the forces of darkness, in wave after seemingly endless wave across both ethereal and mortal planes, was relentless. Azrael's Servitor forces stood their ground valiantly, but were nonetheless whittled away little by little, threatening to tip the favor of the war toward Samael. While the army of Azrael was granted to share in the Cosmic Power by the Seraphim Council, the difficulty lay in the crushingly disproportionate numbers. The divisions of Samael understood clearly that if they did not succeed in defeating the regiments of Azrael, they would not get another chance. Samael put every conceivable essence into the field he could muster. For every soldier of Light, there were unthinkable hordes of Wickedness, feasting on their life force. At the current rate, Azrael would not be able to sustain this fresh onslaught, let alone gain the upper hand again, or even push Samael's legions back.

Seeing the rapidly increasing desperation faced by the forces of good, immeasurable numbers of new essences chose to join the ranks alongside Azrael as Servitors, in order to prevent the collapse of Existence. Column upon column began pouring into the ranks, bolstering Azrael's severely depleted ranks. Reluctance was no longer an option. The war for Existence was forcing every essence to come to terms with their individual conviction and dedication to Existence. It became tragically clear that their decision to remain neutral would unquestionably have dire consequences. Inaction and nonpartisanship were no longer an option for any essence. Samael's campaign of unrestricted war on Existence was the spark needed to bring even the most passive essences into the fray.

The boost to Azrael's efforts were sorely needed, tremendously appreciated, and could not have made more of an impact. With the turn of fortunes, and the swelling of new strength in their ranks, the army of the righteous thus had an opportunity to, with renewed vigor and faith, mount their own effective counterattack. Azrael knew that he and his faithful followers would not be presented with another chance to change the tides of war and, therefore, if they were to permanently shift the balance in their favor, he would need to take advantage of his increased numbers for a bold plan. The fear generated within Azrael by his growing desperation was very real. The intense heartbreak over failing Creation was strong enough, but the notion that the mortal he now loved, who had lost her life so tragically and prematurely, without him having a chance to avenge her, was something he could not bear. Azrael channeled that fear and desperation into an audacious counter-insurgency plan.

Samael's battle plans, as it turned out, provided the very solution Azrael needed in order to reassert control over the outcome of the ongoing war, and eventually provide the chance to defeat the armies of Samael for good. There was one strategy available to Azrael that could prove decisive. That was to challenge Samael over the life force of lost essences and mortal creatures, in his own kind of total war. A total war of righteousness. A revelation came to Azrael that all of the mortal beings destroyed by the forces of Samael could potentially be brought back, the physical frame reanimated with their life forces. Azrael's armies would bring about the reincarnation of every essence or creature that had heretofore been eliminated by Samael's forces. The newly formulated primary objectives would be to bring back to life as many terrestrial creatures that were unjustly destroyed by Samael's ranks, while at the same time continuing to seek out and destroy the malevolent entities, the Keres, the defilements created by Samael to do his disastrous bidding. Azrael determined that this would inevitably be the most effective way of reversing the trajectory of power tipping toward Samael's faction and, therefore, have the effect of rebalancing the fates of Existence. If successful, the battalions of good would not only be able to restore precious life back to mortality but would have an exponentially increasing number of essences among their ranks.

On the other hand, if Azrael's plan failed, if he miscalculated by even a small margin, Samael and the hordes of evil would finish rampaging across the Universe and bring about the final collapse of Existence. The idea was in no way guaranteed success. The decision before Azrael, unfortunately, was not so much a choice as a necessity. They would pursue any means at their disposal.

The retaliation of Samael and those behind his banner proved to be merely short lived, and once again the tide was changing toward a restoration of harmony of balance within Existence. Samael would never again come close to gaining the upper hand. The tides of war would remain in favor of Azrael.

Chapter 20

Within less than a flash of time and space, Azrael, his Servitors, and the other determined hosts of the Heavens had stretched out into every possible reach of Existence, to begin their attempt to turn the tides against Samael and the servants of evil. Detaining the being Samael, and ultimately seeking restitution for his crimes against Eternity, was the mission Azrael had personally set for himself.

It was painfully clear to Azrael that, in pursuing these ends, the very fragile fabric of Existence, the weak bindings thereof, could possibly be torn asunder. Nevertheless, he also understood that to not act would have the exact same unfortunate outcome, and so determined that to try was the only course of action. The other equally unfortunate reality he had to face was the knowledge that the sheer scale of this conflict meant that the losses across the Cosmos would be potentially unimaginable. The inevitability of having to permanently eliminate beings under the command of Samael was a tremendous weight on Azrael, but a burden he was willing to carry. All energy signatures, no matter their particular karma, play a crucial, if even a sacred, role in Existence. Azrael, therefore, understandably felt the full gravity of his predicament. The irony of the situation was also not lost on him. Regrettably, in order to save Existence, he would have to direct the elimination of some of what constituted Existence.

All the more reason to not fail, Azrael thought to himself. *So, that this detestable sacrifice will not be in vain.*

✳ ✳ ✳ ✳ ✳ ✳ ✳ ✳ ✳

Adjacent to the freshly disturbed soil, the evidence of all that remained of a mass grave, hastily dug and provided for hundreds of mortal creatures that had recently been massacred by the minions of Samael, stood a singular entity of Creation amongst the dreadful silence. One of Azrael's Servitors remained motionless, pondering for a split moment, then proceeded with his urgent task.

The mysterious apparition moved a bit closer toward the resting place of the now deceased terrestrial beings, and in an almost unintelligibly soft voice, uttered, "I approach to witness thee."

Slowly bending down, the Servitor grasped for a small handful of soil covering the mass grave, and while still in a crouched position began to gently sprinkle the loose grains of earth back over the spot from which the soil had been initially lifted, staring at the dirt lumps as they fell one by one.

The heavenly companion then arose and lifted up four jars of water which had been previously set upon the ground beside him. Once standing upright, he proceeded to walk slowly around the perimeter of the site of the mass grave, repeating the revolution precisely four times and each time repeating the incantation, "Thy purification is the purification of Life. Drink thee hence the Water of Life. The Heavens will purify thee therewith."

Once again, the Servitor squatted down alongside the mass gravesite, only this time it was to exchange the jars of water for a jar of natron.[76] In precisely the same fashion as it had with the jars of water, the entity en-circled the hastily covered remains of the rotting corpses four more times whilst casting bits of natron out across the field of the dead, and each time reciting, "Oh, offspring of Existence! May ye taste the fullness of the Energy of Life. Partake thee of the fruits of Heaven, the very matter of the Universe. Thy mouth is cleansed, your sustenance is the purification of Life, oh offspring of Creation.'

For the third time, the cosmic companion walked a path around the space in which lay the remains of corporeal creatures for another four times. This time he did so whilst waving a sky-cleaver, and proclaiming the following words, "Be ye purified, Life is purified, be ye purified, Life is purified, be ye purified, Life is purified, be ye purified, Life is purified.[77] Thine cleansing binds thee once again with Existence. Thine mouth is that of a nursing calf. Suckle once again from the breast milk of Life."

Upon completing the third cycle with the sky-cleaver, the Servitor replaced the sky-cleaver in his right hand with a sweet-smelling incense, and continued around the gravesite four more times, speaking an additional set of phrases.

"Be ye censed, Life is censed, be ye censed, Life is censed, be ye censed, Life is censed, be ye censed, Life is censed. Thy censing is thy karma. Be ye censed, be ye censed, be ye censed. Be ye once again reunited with thy mortal brethren. Thy head is censed, thy speech is censed, ye be purified. Receive unto thee once again the Energy of Life. May its scent reach thy nose."

Once he completed the latest circuit around the buried corpses, he paused momentarily, looking out over the expanse of earth before it. Then he finished the sacred incantations for which he had come to give.

"I have come as thine advocate with Creation. I have opened your mouths to once again receive animation. I have balanced thine bones for thee to support thyself. I have marked thine eye for you." And, with a sound as that of a tremendous boom or roar of thunder rolling violently across the sky, the Servitor commanded, "Be ye now filled with the Energy of the Cosmos and rise once more to inhabit this mortal plain."

Utter silence returned once the last syllable was spoken. Not a singular audible sound could have been detected. The Servitor, positioned by the mass grave, called out, though not in a voice perceptible by any physical being, "What are thine names?"

With that, a response was given that only the Servitor could recognize. Resonating from the very depths of the soil, came, "Flesh and blood are our names. They have forever, and will forever, be known to Creation." Instantaneously, the Life Energy of each and every mortal creature therein returned to their respective carbon shells. Life was restored to life.[78]

Then the loose earth covering the mass grave began to stir, imperceptibly so. At first the movement among the grains of soil was barely noticeable. Gradually, however, that movement turned into a growing rumbling, and eventually became an orchestra of geyser-like explosions as dirt began somehow to fling into the air. The stirring lasted only a few moments but culminated in what were hundreds of newly reanimated creatures rising and crawling slowly from their previous subterranean slumber.

The beings that emerged created a terrific scene. One might easily confuse the bewildered, stumbling, moaning, and filthy bodies for the undead, were it not for the undeniable reality that these mortals were once again fully alive and breathing.

After observing the reincarnated terrestrials stumbling about each other in a temporary state of amnesia, the otherworldly companion ended his stay with one last admonishment. "Ye have reemerged into being in thy strength. Ye have been resurrected into being with the sustenance of Life. Sharpness be thine; glory be thine; homage be thine; power be thine. Thine mouth and eyes have been reopened for thee. Go now and live out the remainder of thy mortal existence in peace."[79]

This scene was played out throughout the Universe, across all time and space, by unmeasurable numbers of the faithful defenders of Existence.

✳ ✳ ✳ ✳ ✳ ✳ ✳ ✳ ✳

Though there were only a relative portion of the living things in this and other realms remaining to even possibly take notice, another one of Azrael's many loyal Servitors, having performed the various rites, rituals, and sacred ceremonies to perfection with a tremendous care for their special purposes, went about her thankless mission with as much haste as could be conceivably mustered. There was an insurmountable challenge ahead for her, and others like her, and time was of the essence.

While perhaps unnoticed by mere mortal creatures, the faithful Servitor unfortunately did not remain entirely unobserved. On the contrary, other essences became keenly interested and aware of these activities, and equally as determined to intercede to prevent them. A horde of devilish Keres came upon the scene whilst roaming about the Universe, hunting down and annihilating the soldiers of Creation. Careful as to not give away their presence, the fiends remained inconspicuous, choosing rather to wait and increase their numbers before ultimately attacking.

When their strength was sufficiently gathered and they were confident that they had a force sizable enough to overwhelm and overpower a solitary Servitor, regardless of its cosmic strength, they rushed in. The Keres moved in for the kill like a swarm of angry bees, attacking with such speed and ferocity that the Servitor had virtually no hope of mounting any effort of defending herself. It was an absolute ambush. Before she even knew precisely what was happening, the Keres were upon her, ripping, tearing, and devouring her Life Force.

And as quickly as they had attacked the now extinguished Servitor, and with as much cold disregard, the Keres moved off in countless directions toward countless realms to continue their black deeds.

$$\bigstar\bigstar\bigstar\bigstar\bigstar\bigstar\bigstar\bigstar\bigstar\bigstar$$

Not all attempts made by Azrael's Servitors to revive murdered mortals were successful. Azrael's stratagem did not unfortunately remain unnoticed very long. Almost as quickly as the Servitors began performing the necessary rituals and ordinances necessary for reincarnation, the Keres responded by attacking the faithful servants of Existence, disrupting the sacred sacraments that would have otherwise brought about restoration of life to millions of lost beings. Those initiating the observances for migrating souls back to their former terrestrial shells were exposed and vulnerable to attack while doing so.

Despite the many successful attempts to thwart Azrael's brave allies, Samael and his minions did too little too late. Azrael had enough essences within his ranks to redirect and properly reinforce those Servitors that needed protection while performing the ceremonies of revitalization.

Chapter 21

There are countless learned individuals falsely claiming to have knowledge that one of the undeniable truths, or steadfast principles that governs the mortal plane, is the idea that the forces of energy governing the material or physical realm react in opposition to corresponding initial actions. The same can, and must, be said of more than just characteristics of energy, for matter is energy, and energy is substance, both at the same time and along innumerable dimensions of realities. The very laws of the ethereal govern the physical as well.

Perhaps it was simply foolhardiness that Azrael did not consider the inevitable counter reactions that were expected to occur as a result of such widespread manipulations of the goings on about the mortal plane. Or, possibly, he recognized full well, and adequately anticipated the unstoppable domino effect that would result from interference with the timeline of Creation on such a colossal scale, and, nevertheless, chose to take action, understanding that the ultimate good outweighed the potential consequences. Regardless, the widespread celestial involvement of so many realms of mortality, specifically, and especially, with the mass resurrections of deceased beings, set off a firestorm of unrest and calamity among corporeal creatures.

Virtually every collective species of temporal beings has a belief that there are divine beings of various sorts, be they gods or God, which have and continually intercede on behalf of and in the affairs of they, the mortals. Therefore, and not surprisingly, some of these very same groups saw the large numbers of creatures initially being wiped out by something yet unexplained, only to be brought back just as dramatically, and just as mysteriously, as overwhelming proof of such divine involvement by these assorted respective deities.

In some cases, these physical beings, in their utterly imperfect grasp of the overall greater truth, foolishly perceived what they were witnessing was nothing other than some version of the end of their world, an apocalypse, and – later – that of the beginning of an everlasting peace. They professed that the events collectively witnessed were, in fact, nothing short of the fulfillment of recorded prophecies described in their traditions, written down in sacred texts, or otherwise passed generation to generation orally, stretching back to the beginning of creation. Some accounts, they would claim, told of how, in the end of their world, the mortal remains of the departed would be commanded to rise from the ashes of their eternal slumber, and once again inhabit their physical body and walk the terrestrial realm of the living. Such traditions go on to further describe, in some instances, how a savior, a defender of righteous mortal beings, would be deserving of the credit for bringing about this final and everlasting peace, while forever destroying the souls of wicked creatures.

It is, therefore, understandable, though quite tragically misguided, that the corporeal beings' ignorance was leading them to panic over the events they were experiencing. With no proper understanding of the outrageous nature of the circumstances across Existence, let alone their own insignificant role within Creation, mortals fell into mass hysteria in every part of Creation.

✷✷✷✷✷✷✷✷✷

Many of the self-proclaimed or collectively chosen leaders

of the more cognitively evolved and aware creatures that also profess authority in guiding their species spiritually, or in the matters of things unexplainable, stood upon their high places, and lifted their voices up so that they might receive the singular recognition that they alone could guide their fellow beings through to a kind of salvation of the body and soul. These very same individuals, and those beings they convinced to organize together as bodies of faithful followers, sought to distinguish themselves from others, others that they argued were, for one reason or another, not worthy, or as worthy, of surviving the end of the world, and thus inheriting a perfected existence.

These foolish falsehoods spread more quickly than a flame does when sparked in a pile of dry underbrush. Brothers accused brothers, sisters turned on sisters, accusing each other of unforgivable wickedness and heresy, and of not being a properly consecrated soul. Parents cast out children and children disavowed parents over what they saw were the inequities of the other, based solely on the shallow utterances of a few from their kind that claimed to have been initiated in some kind of ill-conceived partnership with a god or gods. Individuals and even communities as a whole felt justified and empowered to pass widespread judgment upon any and all that did not necessarily share a similar ideology, declaring moral superiority.

Precisely because mortal beings do not, and simply cannot, grasp the deeper or broader nature of the circumstances faced across the vastness of Creation, these beings were unfortunately left to their own devices for interpreting conditions. Their ignorance contributed ultimately to utter confusion and endless mass hysteria. Many terrestrials believed that what they were witnessing was profound evidence of something like an end of days or final divine reckoning. In the absence of eternal truths, the untruths would perpetuate and feed even more false dogma.

✳✳✳✳✳✳✳✳✳

Azrael was not blind to what was transpiring among the multitudes of creatures for whom, in part, he was defending Existence. On the contrary, rather, he was sufficiently concerned. Nevertheless, in the end, the material manifestations of the Energy of Life were merely that. The Balance of Existence would be eternally, and singularly, the only consideration. He fully believed, nay, placed unwavering faith in the concept that once balance was returned to Creation, that very same harmony would find its way into the physical realm once again.

Azrael thought of Johanna. No matter how blasphemous his feelings were on the subject, it was a small consolation that her mortal existence would be safe from much of the chaos and tribulation of others of her kind, until such time as he could restore her life force once again within its material shell.

It begins as a breeze; gentle, calm, like a whisper from an intimate friend. It makes every effort to touch all things before moving quietly bye. There is no evidence of even the mildest of sounds created by its movement. Slowly...slowly... with the knowledge of every form and dimension it glides along effortlessly. It cools, comforts, and relaxes the sinews.

Unknown Source[81]

Chapter 22

Despite Azrael's extensive wisdom from his experience and longevity as an essence, and Samael's cunning, both failed to grasp one very critical principle of Existence. Outcomes are never certain. The inevitable is by nature not in actuality inevitable, but, rather, entirely uncertain. Both had their own respective expectations and desired conclusions to circumstances. Nevertheless, what they failed to comprehend was that in reality they had absolutely no influence on the occurrences of time and space.

"*Observe that which is observable. All play their parts. Allow what is to be,*" echoed the collective energy of the Seraphim Council.

There was a reason why the Sacred Council did not get directly involved in the fortunes facing Existence.

They recognized the universal truth that it did not have even a modest role in any fates that lay before Existence. If Existence was in fact doomed to collapse into nothingness, it was, is, and would effectually be its destiny.

✷✷✷✷✷✷✷✷✷

For far too much space in time, and at the cost of exceeding numbers of essences, the struggle between the forces of darkness was waged, led by the energy in form known as Samael, and those who dared to challenge them against all conceivable odds, the allies of light under Azrael. In every corner of the Universe the suffering was tragic, catastrophic. The cosmic conflict caused the very framework of time and space to begin to fracture and tear and may very well have led to the eventual collapse of Existence, regardless of anything perpetrated by Samael and his minions. The life forces of countless beings, whether abominable or not, were lost to Eternity, and the energy of immeasurable essences were sadly wiped forever from the Annals of Existence. There was no honor or glory...only tragedy without perceptible limits.

In the end, however, and despite the absolutely overwhelming odds, it was fated that Existence would remain for eternity. The abominations of Samael began to abandon the cause in droves, choosing instead to hide in whichever dark crack in the Cosmos they could find, rather than face the inevitable fate in store for them. Their sense of terror as they fled the battlefields was noxious. A small number of the more resolved among Samael's ranks, however, tried in last efforts of desperation to resist, only to have the last measure of their reality cut from them. The few that continued fighting did so haphazardly. Azrael's forces exploited the chaos among Samael's ranks, working to eliminate the last remaining vestiges of evil with surgical precision and coordination. There was, however, no refuge for the wicked, no rest for the damned. With the Keres in full retreat across the Universe, the Servitor forces made the final push towards victory. Exercising the full limits of cosmic power gifted to them, they bound and confounded the life energy of any and all remaining evil essences. Those Keres that chose to surrender were gathered for eventual judgment by the Great Council. They would never threaten Existence again. Azrael, and the many unwaveringly faithful Servitors by his side, ultimately prevailed against the unholy forces of Samael.

Chapter 23

If there ever were a moment in time and space in which the word silence could be offered as an accurate description for the overall state of the Universe, this was that instance. Every carbon form within the physical realm, every child of Creation, from the most microscopic single-celled organisms to the largest creatures, all felt a collective sense of profound calm; so strong that it was as if they could literally feel comforted by its invisible embrace. Disappointingly, of course, these beings would never know the tragic circumstances that occurred behind this momentary sense of euphoria. No less spectacular was the intense surge of energy that pulsed throughout the immeasurable numbers of cosmic essences about the Ethereal Plane. The difference, however, was, of course, that these selfless and brave servants of Existence were intimately and profoundly aware of why they were suddenly overcome by such a magnificently positive sensation. Existence was meant to prevail.

"*Harmony...cosmic harmony!*" declared the Seraphim Council.

While the sacred balance between dark and light had ultimately been restored, the arduous, yet necessary, steps along the healing process had only just begun. The lingering scars left behind by the conflict, hence, to be referred to as the Great Cosmic War, were limitless, and sadly the repercussions of that damage would not be fully recognized for millennia upon millennia, if ever. Nonetheless, and for at least this point in space and time, regardless of all else, there was peace; *pax aeterna.*

There were tears within the fabric of time space which needed to heal. Rogue agents of Samael were still at large and needed to be rounded up for final judgment. The corporeal realm was in utter chaos. These were, nevertheless, merely temporary setbacks. All would once again be made right across Existence.

✳✳✳✳✳✳✳✳✳

Given the hard fought, yet ultimate success of the cosmic campaign to restore Balance about Existence, one could easily forgive Azrael for choosing to make his presence scarce for a considerable length of time. No individual essence had ever hitherto earned or deserved such a respite more than he had. Nonetheless, Azrael could not, or perhaps rather, would not, allow himself to rest. Not so long as there was still one remaining task of singular importance for Azrael: that of reanimating Johanna's physical frame with her life energy. He made this clear to the Servitors, who alongside him had to continue restoring mortality to countless beings, that he, and he alone, would see to her resurrection.

While Johanna was not the reason for which Azrael bravely took upon himself the daunting mantle of responsibility and risk of standing up to Samael's dark forces, she was certainly every bit the inspiration his essence needed to drive him forward. Her memory was a boulder of courage upon which he often leaned for support whenever he felt his resolve challenged or weakened. Azrael felt duty bound, as well as love bound, to be the essence that restored Life back to Johanna; especially since it was likely to be the last instance for which his essence would ever be allowed to have contact with her ever again. There could be no sweeter or more appropriate parting gesture.

Standing, leaning slightly to his right side against the inside of the door frame, Azrael peered into the silent space within Johanna's bedchamber. The brilliant rays of the midday sun illuminated every corner of the room, including the lifeless remains of Johanna's physical frame, undisturbed, just as it had been when her life force was so violently ripped from her, lying in innocence in her bed.

Azrael thought to himself, *Even in death and decay she is still a tremendously beautiful creature.*

Finally accepting and admitting fully to his feelings on the matter, Azrael, for the very first time, allowed himself to openly explore the nature of his affection for the formerly mortal woman lying before him. The terrible experiences he had had as of late brought a powerful realization, that there was nothing he should or need to fear, including love… especially love. Even if that meant facing another eventual and certain cosmic punishment.

Moving slowly, yet with a great sense of purpose, Azrael took a few steps across the room over to the side of Johanna's bed. After pausing briefly, he sat down beside her pale and motionless body, his gaze never leaving her, even for a moment. With his new awareness of confidence, Azrael was emboldened to reach his hand forward and gently ran the right hand of the physical form he was assuming through the silky, long blonde locks of Johanna's hair. The texture stirred an electric sensation within him. Memories – wonderful glimpses of their few fleeting moments together – flooded through his consciousness. Azrael found it impossible to hold back the stream of tears that first welled up, and then subsequently began rolling down his cheeks. These were not tears of sadness, though. Rather, they were of tremendous exultation.

For a time, Azrael allowed himself to bask in the freedom that this rare emotional release was providing his essence. The exercise in bathing in this mortal out-pouring of emotions, as he remembered quite well, was immensely cathartic. Besides, there was no point in holding back any longer. If there was ever an essence in Existence that had ever earned the right to feel as a carbon creature does, he had. Therefore, he relished the moment, soaking in every sensation to the fullest, for he had nothing if not infinite time and space to do so now.

When he reached the point at which he felt he had indulged his mortal tendencies enough and was sufficiently prepared emotionally and spiritually to proceed with the originally intended nature of the visitation, Azrael gathered himself in order to begin the sacred rite and ritual for restoring Johanna's life energy to the terrestrial frame it once inhabited.

Thus, he began, "Arise for me, Johanna; stand up for me. It is I; I am thy servant; I am Azrael. I have come to thee, that I may purify thee, that I may cleanse thee, that I may revive thee, that I may reanimate for thee thy mortal shell. For I am Azrael, the avenger of Existence. I have smitten for thee him who smote thee; I have avenged thee, my dearest Johanna, on him who did thee evil. I have come to thee by order of Existence."[82]

Azrael paused only briefly before resuming once again the solemn incantation. "Thy energy belongs to thee, thine abundance belongs to thee, thine efflux belongs to thee, which issues from Existence. Collect thy bones; arrange thy limbs; shake off thy dust. The tomb is open for thee; the doors of Life are once again open to thee. Thy soul is once again in thy body; thy might is behind thee; remain chief of thy powers. Raise thyself up, Johanna; be thou powerful over the powers that are in thee."[83]

Immediately upon finishing the last syllable of the ritual, Johanna's carbon form suddenly lifted chest first off of the bed, back arched, and head hanging backward. With mouth wide open as in desperate anticipation to receive something, Johanna's mortal frame gasped and shivered ferociously and deeply for air – a vital necessity long since denied to it. The first breaths were convulsive and violent. Nevertheless, Johanna's newly reanimated body showed clear signs of gradually regaining full control of its ability to inhale and exhale properly. She did not regain consciousness immediately, however, and it was perhaps better that way. Azrael was not sure how he would handle their reunion. He was content, therefore, to keep vigil over the fragile condition of his beloved in the meantime.

Chapter 24

The newly revived terrestrial form of Johanna, her life force and carbon shell having been reunited, remained unconscious for some time in her bed, and Azrael made absolutely no effort to disturb her rest. He knew she would eventually revive on her own. Otherwise, she showed all of the necessary vital signs of a mortal being in fantastic health. At no point did Azrael become concerned about the physical condition of this creature for which he cared so deeply. Nevertheless, his patience was challenged, for despite wanting so desperately to actually see Johanna rise again, he was forced to accept certain realities of the nature of reanimation. Things needed to happen on their own timeline.

Azrael did find some amusement in the notion that, as a celestial essence accustomed to infinite spaces of time, he was behaving like a petulant child, unable to pass such a relatively short amount of time without agitation. He was not going anywhere soon, and Johanna was not either, for that matter. In the end, Azrael came to the realization that the fact that he could even have the opportunity to once again see this amazing creature alive was in and of itself enough of a blessing. Azrael had no more inklings of impatience ever after.

At first, Azrael chose to stay seated on the side of the bed, just as he had until she had been reanimated. Eventually, however, he migrated to a relatively rickety and somewhat unstable wooden chair a few feet across the room from the bed. There he sat, in absolute dead silence, maintaining a diligent and undistracted vigil over his beloved.

Azrael could never recall precisely how much time had passed – perhaps a day, perhaps two, or several – when Johanna did finally regain consciousness. In the end, it certainly did not matter. All that mattered was that she did.

It began with the occasional, random twitch of a finger or toe, and a weak, guttural groan. This lasted on and off for a little while. Ever so gradually, though, and with increasing strength and vitality, she began shifting and turning about restlessly. Without a fraction of hesitation, Azrael leapt out of the chair, and back next to Johanna's awakening body in great anticipation. Finally, her eyelids peaked open with a slight crack, slowly at first, then they widened more, until eventually they were wide open and blinking. With her pupils still dilated, and in a fog of confusion, Johanna lay silently looking up toward the ceiling, her mouth slightly ajar. As her vision was restored, so too was her interest in establishing an awareness of her surroundings.

Initially, she was only able to tilt her head side to side in slow, awkward movements. When that did not satisfy her desperation for reacclimating to her immediate environs, she determined to get up somehow.

The first several attempts to bring her arms up under her sides and lift herself up were defeating and unsuccessful. Her arms, like much of the rest of her body, were still just beginning to regain a margin of sensation. When Johanna could finally prop herself up on her elbows and peer forward, inching upward as she did, she was immediately brought face to face with Azrael, who, not wanting to intercede in her recovery, sat by her side, waiting patiently.

A mixture of emotions, ranging from tremendous confusion, affection, great concern, sadness, terror, longing, and elation, all flooded instantaneously through Johanna's heart and mind, in a continual cycle. Without even realizing it, her jaw went slack even more than it had been, opening her mouth even more, and revealing her obvious shock. Tears began to well up and then dribble down her still slightly pale cheeks, uncontrollably, as a natural response to all that she was thinking and feeling. Azrael looked upon Johanna with a tenderness that only comes from someone in love and reached out with his right hand to lightly brush away the fresh tears.

As Azrael's fingers gently glanced across her cheeks, Johanna, almost from a dormant instinct, reached up with her left hand and seized his wrist with an unusual strength. She pulled Azrael toward her with all of the energy she could muster at that moment, transitioning both of her arms around his shoulders in a firm, yet loving embrace. Azrael immediately reciprocated by leaning in and reaching his arms around Johanna, squeezing slightly, a little unsure of how fragile her condition may still have been. They remained locked together as one, neither having the slightest desire to let the other go. If both could have had their wishes granted in that instance, they would have melded into one being, and remained as such for eternity.

Despite wanting to stay perpetually in each other's arms, nevertheless, Johanna and Azrael both accepted that it was also not realistic. They knew that at some point they would have to face reality once again. Almost in unison, the two felt that it was time, and slowly moved apart until they were looking at each other once again. For Johanna, this was the first time since before her untimely demise that she had been able to look upon this man for whom she was madly in love. In his arms, Azrael felt that Johanna's muscles were tense and rigid, not yet ready to relax. He also recognized, though, that it was to be expected of someone who had recently been through as much trauma as Johanna had.

Johanna would understandably have hundreds of questions. No, more accurately, she would need or even crave the answers to those questions as mortal creatures require nourishment. It came almost as a surprise just how overwhelming that necessity felt. Thoughts, words, and feelings were all bubbling to the surface at once, competing with each other for priority. Despite trying to calm herself down, in the end there was little she could do to keep it all from flooding out.

In an unexpected and sudden explosion of sound, Johanna blurted out, "WWWWHAT HAAAAAPPENED?!!!"

As soon as the words had left her lips, she shrank back in embarrassment, taking her eyes off of Azrael as she glanced away, feeling extremely foolish for how awkward she sounded. Unperturbed and unbothered by anything she could possibly say or do, Azrael maintained his composure. Instead, he simply widened his smile in response, almost in an instinctual effort to reassure Johanna.

There was one lingering obstacle on Azrael's mind, however. That of how to best discuss or explain things with Johanna and answer the myriad questions she would inevitably throw at him. This was an obviously new experience for him, and one he did not look forward to facing. *How does one explain to a terrestrial being such as Johanna the kinds of things necessary in order for them to have even a marginal comprehension or appreciation of what transpired across Existence? Is it even possible for such imperfect beings to grasp in some small measure enough to make sense of the magnitude of events about which they have no awareness? If the answer to those questions was an astounding yes, would it ultimately even make a difference whether she knew all that had transpired? Should I leave out certain details? If so, which ones? Would it be best to simplify my explanation? Should I lie to her in order to try to save her from potential anguish and heartache? If I do, the likelihood was that Johanna would see right through the attempt and feel hurt as a result.* In the end, Azrael decided, or rather reluctantly convinced himself, that the best course would be to lay it all out for her, and let come what may.

Johanna spoke again. This time, though, she was able to muster much more control over her faculties and was thus able to speak with some composure. "What are you doing here? I.... I mean.... what happened? Something isn't right. Or.... rather....my head....my body...." Johanna began looking around, her eyes darting as she did so. "I feel.... confused. No, not confused.... I...." Dropping her head to her chest now, Johanna began to cry again, and added, "What's wrong with me? Why are you here?"

The bewilderment was intense, and very real. Azrael could clearly sense that. While he had anticipated that there would obviously be a period of adjustment, he had no idea how long or how unsettling it would, or could, ultimately be for Johanna, or for the rest of mortal kind, for that matter. He could only hope for the best. But seeing her in obvious emotional discomfort, he gently lifted her chin up until her gaze was once again locked with his. The gesture had the intended effect because her heartbeat slowed a measure, and she stopped crying. Instead, she just looked into Azrael's eyes, waiting for some sort of response that would bring her some measure of peace.

The moment was now. Azrael could not put off what he expected to be an extremely uncomfortable and perhaps overwhelming conversation. "Johanna, my dear, there are things.... there are things which I must share with you. These will not be easy for you to hear, nor I'm afraid, will they make much sense. Nonetheless, you deserve to hear them, and from me alone."

Azrael began by asking Johanna what she remembered prior to reawakening in her bed. Johanna's reply was, of course, that she could not remember anything out of the ordinary, just that she had been in her room. Proceeding, Azrael informed Johanna that she had in fact died, and then further shared with her the terrible circumstances and events which corresponded with why she had died in the first place. Having sat up in her bed perfectly quietly, Johanna assumed the posture of someone that thought they were ready to absorb hard to swallow information. Despite appearances, however, Azrael could clearly feel how challenging and gut wrenching it was for Johanna to accept what she was being told. Her form was rigid, tensing up, with every muscle in her body seizing up again. Nevertheless, she never betrayed how uncomfortable she was, or how impossible it was to believe her ears, with the exception of her hands occasionally shaking. Johanna sat bravely and resolutely, and absolutely attentive to Azrael's every word.

Trying to be as detailed, yet sensitive, as possible, and, assuming some things would inevitably be left out unintentionally, Azrael tried to provide an accurate and complete account. He was sure to apologize for not being completely forthright with her in their first interactions but assured her that there were obvious reasons for the discretion. It was necessary, of course, to divulge who he was, what he was, and his role in what had befallen her.

Azrael revealed that, though once a mortal being such as she, he was no longer so, but was now an eternal servant of Existence. This included a rather awkward and clumsy attempt to explain how he, a celestial essence, was and is able to take the form of a mortal creature, and thus interact with other terrestrial beings.[84]

Continuing to take everything in stride, Johanna, to Azrael's surprise, never once interjected or interrupted for any reason. He considered that a sign that he should simply continue. Azrael could not help but think, though, that this was the quiet before the storm. Or, the lack of responsiveness was more from emotional and spiritual shock, than from anything else.

When he came to a natural point of conclusion, Azrael addressed Johanna, "I do believe that I have talked for long enough. It would do me a great deal of good to hear from you."

Johanna, however, said nothing. She showed no signs of wanting to respond at all. Rather, she turned to look down to her right, toward the shabby wooden floorboards. Aside from the occasional sigh, she remained relatively silent, almost lost in a daydream of sorts. Then, suddenly, she broke the embrace she had maintained with Azrael, and began working her legs out from under the sheets, struggling a bit in the process. When Azrael understood that she meant to get out of bed, he shifted himself back to the end of the bed so that she would be unimpeded. Johanna did, in fact, get out of bed. And when she had, the first thing she did was shuffle slowly and gingerly across the floor a few steps and stand beside the window, staring out at the fading light of dusk. There she stood for several minutes, leaning against the window where the pane met the frame, as if something outside were more riveting at that moment than what she had been told, and had drawn her undivided attention away with it. Azrael made no attempt to get Johanna to speak. There was no need.

"Why are you here?" she abruptly asked, while still not making eye contact.

Azrael was quite understandably taken back by the question. While he was certainly expecting to be questioned and was even prepared perhaps for Johanna to express some anger, he was not anticipating this. Additionally, it was not clear to him the context in which Johanna was asking and, therefore, he found himself struggling to form a response.

Not willing to wait any longer for a reply, Johanna repeated herself. Turning now to look upon him, she asked, with noticeable seriousness, "Why are you here?"

She was not asking him out of anger or otherwise. It was clear to Azrael that there was something entirely different behind her words, anguish, confusion, sorrow.

Trying to understand the reasoning behind the

question, he attempted to reply, but instead of sharing what he really felt, he said, "I am here in order for you to be reunited as One, body and soul. I believed...."

"No, why are *you* here?" Johanna interrupted, as she turned to look out the window once more. "There are many things about all of this that are simply beyond me." She motioned with her left hand, in a waving pattern. "I can accept that I may never understand even a fraction of what I heard. Perhaps it is even best that way. But from what you have told me, there were countless, how did you put it, essences, reviving those like me. Any one of them could have been tasked with me. Any one of them. But you chose to come. You didn't need to remain with me, but you did, nonetheless. Instead of allowing me blissful ignorance, you shared all, knowing full well that it would largely be incomprehensible to me. So, I ask again, why have *you* come?"

It was now perfectly clear to Azrael what Johanna had meant all along.

"You have asked the wrong question. I believe you want to know why I am *still* here?" Azrael clarified, before continuing, "I can read what's in your heart. You want to know whether I am here to stay, or whether this is my way of saying goodbye? You want to know.... if this is the final goodbye?"

Johanna turned to him, and Azrael instantly saw

in the moist glimmer of her eyes that that was precisely what she wanted to know. It was impossible to prevent his own eyes from watering up in response. Stretching his arms out toward her, Azrael gestured for Johanna to return to the bed and rejoin him. She did so. He took her hands in his, squeezing them ever so tenderly.

Azrael pondered for a moment whether or not he had the courage to share his true feelings with Johanna. In the end, and with tremendous trepidation and difficulty, he decided that it was best to withhold his true feelings, even in this moment. He reasoned with himself that divulging such feelings would serve no purpose other than to lead to utter heartache, and he could not or would not be the cause of breaking her heart. Besides, he told himself that, in an effort to convince himself of the virtue of his decision, Johanna had already sensed the truth for herself. There was ultimately no possibility for a cosmic essence such as he to ever be allowed happiness again with a mortal woman and, therefore, no reason to get caught up entertaining such a fanciful notion. If Johanna were honest with herself, she too would come to the exact same disappointing, yet inevitable conclusion.

"Now that you know who and what I am, you also know that I cannot linger in the mortal realm, let alone remain for any time with you," Azrael said.

Johanna looked deeply into his eyes, as if intentionally stealing a few more moments with him, then nodded her head, demonstrating that she did, unfortunately, and disappointingly, understand. The fact that she understood did not mean that she was not painfully depressed at the thought that this was to be their last time together. And it did not prevent the tears from streaming uncontrollably. It was painfully clear to Azrael that he needed to depart sooner rather than later, so as to not prolong the anguish either of them was, or would, feel.

"Johanna, my beloved – if I may refer to you as such – I do wish things between us could be under different circumstances. Mine must be an existence of loneliness, forever in the chains of emptiness.[85] Be assured, however, that I will be watching over you, and you will never be forgotten, ever. Look for me in your dreams, where we will always have each other.[86] And when that fateful time arrives for your leaf to fall from the Tree of Life, I will be there to retrieve it. It will be I by your side, ready to per-sonally guide you back home," concluded Azrael.[87]

At this point, Johanna was beside herself, almost convulsing with fits of crying while also gasping for air. Reaching out with both hands and cupping Johanna's cheeks softly, Azrael leaned in closer. Her tearful spasms began to subside slowly, until it was nothing more than an occasional sniffle. Then she reciprocated the gesture by taking Azrael by the cheeks. Connected with each other in an unflinching gaze, and pulled together by a powerful magnetism, Azrael and Johanna finally came together in unison, locking lips in a passionate kiss. The raw energy which radiated from the contact between these two was unfathomable. There was never, or ever would be, a kiss to match its sheer intensity.

Though, and to the supreme disappointment of both, it could not last. When they did eventually separate, Azrael simply stood, looked down with an awkward smile for one last second, and then promptly departed, leaving Johanna in her bedchamber to face the inevitably tumultuous heartache all alone.

88

"There is no man who lives and, seeing the angel of death, can deliver his soul from his hand."

Psalm 89, verse 45

Chapter 25

Never in all the space and time of Existence were there so many eternal essences gathered in and as one singularity. The circumstances, however, were of such a cosmic magnitude, and there was not a single form of energy or terrestrial organism that was not affected to the core by the Great War for Existence, as it would be referred to. The ill effects would be felt for unheard of life cycles still to come. Every cosmic essence that was not eliminated in the horrific ordeal made sure to be present for the proceedings against Samael and his entourage of darkness.

There was one exception, one that chose to remain entirely absent: Azrael. For Azrael, the proceedings held no value or importance. As an essence he had already long since made his peace with the dreadful events and circumstances for which he was fatefully involved.

The Seraphim Council had the unenviable task of dealing with and dispatching galactic justice upon these various essences, though, there was no shortage of anticipation of what the rulings would ultimately be. The Keres and the other forms of demonic energy Samael's followers had taken were brought first before the Council for judgment and sentencing. This was not a trial. This was not a hearing. This was not the courtroom found among some terrestrial creatures in which truth is sought after. The actions of Samael and his hordes of evil were and are eternally recorded and, therefore, were without a shred of doubt. There was only a proclamation of guilt along with a declaration of punishment.

For the onlooking crowds of celestial beings of energy there was absolutely no gratification in the trial itself. They were, however, not in attendance to merely indulge a fanciful wish for ultimate revenge. Rather, they were present out of an overwhelming call of solidarity with Existence, for what they faithfully and unwaveringly served.

In the end, the Great Council issued the decree that all twisted essences that had been in the service of Samael be eliminated for good – eliminated permanently from Creation. There was no collective response from the energy signatures present. The outcome was, while just, equally tragic. The eradication of part of Creation was never, under any circumstances, a desirable conclusion.

The issuance of judgment of primary importance, however, was yet to begin. Samael would eventually meet his final fate.

✳✳✳✳✳✳✳✳✳

"Bring it forth before this council," the holy Seraphim Council pronounced.

There was suddenly what could only be described as a collective hush across the Ethereal Plane as the gathered essences waited in anticipation for the essence known as Samael to be brought forth. When Samael did make his approach, he made no attempt to voice or call out in protest. Instead, he tried his best to present himself as a dignified essence. The holy members of the Seraphim Council allowed a fraction of a moment, expecting something from him. When there was only silence, the great body proceeded.

"You know why you have been brought before this great Council," said the Council in unison. *"What do you say to this?"*

Still nothing came from Samael, except complete obstinance, defiant to the end.

"Then...." continued the Council when it was suddenly interrupted.

Samael finally spoke on his own behalf. "I stood and do stand against the tyranny that is this Council." Expecting some kind of response from the Seraphim Council, or any of the multitude of energies, Samael paused. But the Council was unfazed and unmoved, not dignifying his comments with a reply.

Determined to provoke some kind of reaction, Samael continued, "In my time as a carbon being, I lived according to all of the most righteous principles and precepts of my people. Mine was an existence worthy of remembrance and great celebration. How was my energy rewarded upon the demise of that mortal shell? I was condemned for all eternity as the slave of the most wicked and foul souls of Existence, the final companion of the most despised of the Universe. Azrael, on the other hand, an essence that once betrayed his sacred office, and was punished by this very council for his disobedience, was tasked with guiding the brightest energies. How does this body justify this?"

When the Seraphim Council sensed that Samael had momentarily finished his egotistical rant, it did reply, though, perhaps not as Samael was hoping it would. *"All energy is bound in the service of Existence. It is not to question or justify what is. Existence was, is, and will always be."*

Infuriated by the cryptic rebuttal, Samael lashed out. "Pass sentence then. I look forward to my Fate with exuberant expectation!"

"*As it should be,*" the Council began to proclaim. "*Samael, Son of Existence, for your unwise and misguided deeds, your punishment will be that you are to be restored to your former celestial calling, to serve the Cosmos once more and for eternity, and to do so forever miserable and self-loathing if so chosen.*"

Samael was utterly shocked. This was not the result he had hoped for. He had genuinely desired above all outcomes to have his energy signature eliminated from Existence once and for all, and thus, end the unwarranted suffering he believed was his. Instead, his essence was in a sense being forced by the Fates to come face to face with the very darkness within once again. Had he misunderstood...was that possible? Was he in fact the critical piece? The energy of his essence was the counterbalance, the pendulum swinging proverbially back. He was the Balance.

✷✷✷✷✷✷✷✷✷✷

"*Thus, Harmony and Balance are restored. Merciful are the Fates.*"

Chapter 26

After determining the ultimate resolution of the matter regarding the fate of Samael, there was one last pronouncement the Seraphim Council needed to make – that of how Azrael should be sufficiently recognized for his role in protecting Existence from annihilation. The sacred body recognized that Azrael would never seek out any form of praise for himself. It was simply not in his nature to do so. Nonetheless, the Council felt strongly that Azrael deserved something for his tremendous devotion, and It knew precisely how to honor him.

Azrael was eventually summoned before the Seraphim Council. For what reason, he did not know, though he surmised that it was related to Its judgment and sentencing of Samael. He did not believe the Council would seek to justify Itself. It was above such trivialities. Still, perhaps It sought a reaction in some form from him. Either way, he resolved that he had no opinion or insight on the matter. Samael's fate was his, while he, Azrael, had his own to accept.

When Azrael appeared before the Council of Light, his essence was already anxiously anticipated. *"Azrael, Son of Existence, Loyal Servant of Eternity, your presence honors this council,"* began the Seraphim Council.

"It is I that am honored; honored to be summoned by You," replied Azrael.

"Do you know the reason for which your presence has been requested by this body?" asked the Council.

"Regretfully, I am ignorant of such things. Nevertheless, I am eternally Your humble servant. You have but to ask...." Azrael almost finished speaking before he was cut off.

"No....no.... this Council seeks nothing from you. On the contrary. That which you seek will be henceforth granted to you. Your fate has yet to be revealed to you," interjected the Seraphim Council.

"My fate? I do not understand. Please, forgive my ignorance, but I seek nothing. Especially from this great council."

"*Nay, but there is something you seek, but do not dare speak it. The Ethereal Record has a different story unfolding for you, sweet Azrael. Your path was always destined, it seems, to be otherwise. Go forth.... your fate still lies before you yet waiting to be declared. Peace and love for all of thy days,*" was the last thing the Seraphim Council communicated to Azrael's essence.... ever.

Chapter 27

Life eventually, and quite inevitably, returned to a semblance of normalcy, at least from the outward appearance to the uninitiated. Mortal creatures and creations in all their infinitesimal numbers, shapes, and kinds, in every dimension of time and space, behaved just as should be expected of them, none of which having even the smallest inclination as to the nature of events that so nearly brought an abrupt end to their reality. All except one.

At her request, and against his better judgment, Azrael allowed Johanna to retain a full and unfiltered recollection of every memory and feeling. She had practically begged Azrael to grant her this wish before being separated for the last time. Perhaps it was a curse, perhaps a blessing, perhaps both, and perhaps nothing at all. *Only time will tell,* Johanna kept repeating to herself, largely to convince herself more than anything else.

In the hours and first days after Azrael's final good-bye, Johanna tried desperately to return to her previous routines, if only to fulfill her part in the great illusion that life was moving forward as it always had. Nevertheless, every movement – blinking, breathing, walking – was utter torture for Johanna. She constantly caught herself drifting off in thought and feeling, only to have to drag herself back to the reality of the present. The reality that she would never be able to relate again to anyone or confide in them when the feelings inside became unbearable – not even her parents – and that she had to accept her heartbreak for the rest of her life. Despite how tremendously overwhelming these emotions were for her, often, it felt, boiling over, Johanna would have it no other way. The raw emotions were her burden to bear if she wanted to have any lasting memory at all of the energy that once connected Azrael with her. And she would enthusiastically make the same choice again, and again, till the end of her days.

✶ ✶ ✶ ✶ ✶ ✶ ✶ ✶ ✶ ✶

The noises were all the same. The smells were all the same. The crowds and commotion were all the same. All of the sensations of working at her parents' cafe were exactly the same as they had always been, and likely always would be. One morning Johanna found herself willing herself, even forcing herself, through her daily chores and duties. She felt as though her soul and body were acting in opposition to one another; the body performing the mechanical tasks expected of an ignorant entity trapped physically, while her heart and mind were watching her body, disappointed...ashamed even. Johanna, however, continued about her work, nonetheless.

While wiping down one of the small tables that sat off from the cafe a little into the market square, Johanna felt a sudden, and overwhelming, sensation. At first, she was quite unsure of precisely what she was experiencing. A range of emotions and thoughts raced through her, disorganized and fleeting, as she tried to recognize the cause of this flood of feeling. Then, like a jolt of electricity down the full length of her spine, she had a very clear notion that she was being watched; that there were a pair of eyes on her at that very moment. And there was something incredibly powerful, benevolent, and warmly familiar with this new revelation. The prompting to look up was overpowering, and rather euphoric.

"My love!" a gentle voice called to her. "My love!"

Standing frozen in place, as she had been exactly when first overcome with this all-consuming sensation, still in the motion of tidying up the table, Johanna gradually, and very cautiously lifted her head ever so slightly to her left, in order to face out toward the expanse of the market square, choosing to close her eyes in nervousness as she did so.

Beginning now to breathe quite heavily, Johanna's frame remained locked, and her eyes stayed shut for several moments. Then the soft voice came again. "My love!"

Johanna finally mustered enough of a resolve to open the lids of her eyes, though she did so extremely slowly, millimeters at a time. Once her eyes were completely open, her vision remained relatively out of focus, and needed a fraction of a second to adjust. Nonetheless, when her eyesight had recovered, and she could clearly see out into the square, Johanna's heart instantly stopped, in shock, and, as if followed by the air in her lungs being sucked out through her gaping mouth, so did her breathing. At the same time, her face became flush in bright pink, and her eyes welled up with moisture before it ultimately cascaded down her cheeks in great torrents of tears.

Though it certainly seemed like an eternity, Johanna did inevitably regain full control once again of her faculties, enough to resume breathing, beginning subsequently with a desperate inhalation for air, along with a series of convulsive breaths.

Amongst the bustling crowds of shouting merchants and haggling townsfolk stood the cause of Johanna's over-whelming surprise. There, no more than a mere thirty yards away, gazing and smiling widely back toward her as though there were nothing or no one else within sight, was a familiar face. His physical form was the same as he had assumed all those times whilst in the terrestrial plane – the young man in whom Johanna had fallen deeply in love with, and who had in turn fallen in love with her.

This cannot be... this simply cannot be!, Johanna thought to herself, still breathing quite heavily, her heart pounding in her chest.

Johanna desperately wanted to be wrong, but she was finding the feelings of disbelief were difficult to push aside. This vision of Azrael before her could, she con-jectured, easily be, and likely was, nothing more than a powerful illusion, a simple manifestation of her intense grieved and hyper-emotional condition.

"You are such a silly, foolish girl," she told herself, almost angry with herself for succumbing to what, at that moment, she could only perceive as weakness – weakness brought on, of course, by her heightened emotional state.

But then something rather unexpected happened.

The image of Azrael before her began to move, to take slow and steady steps toward her, maintaining its gaze on her with every one of those steps. Some of the symptoms of shock previously felt returned anew, as Johanna was faced with the rise of the very real possibility that she was not so naive after all. As Azrael's form approached, Johanna was struck with the intensity of realizing for the first time since sensing him that somehow, someway, despite being told under no uncertain terms of the utter impossibility of it, her eternal love had been returned to her. They were as it turned out fated for each other. Instinctually, there was only one thing for Johanna to do, only one thing she wanted to do, and that was to drop everything, and dash toward her love.

Johanna did just that. Without a moment of hesitation, she let the damp rag and dirty cup and saucer in her hands fall awkwardly to the half-cleaned table she had been wiping, and immediately turned and began running with as much speed as she could humanly gather toward Azrael. Once again, warm tears began to pour down her flushed cheeks, though, these were tears of the most immense elation describable.

It only took a mere couple of seconds for Johanna to reach Azrael and, as she did so, he casually outstretched his arms in anticipation for the obvious embrace to follow. When it did come, Johanna did not leap into Azrael's waiting arms so much as she crashed into them. Like two stars colliding into one another, the resulting embrace and kiss that followed was positively nuclear. If the mutual energy produced by the embrace could be visible, it would have been magnificent to behold. The two star-struck lovers remained locked together for some time, neither having any intention of letting the other go, resolved, rather, to forge themselves into one entity with their tremendous passion. No spoken words needed to be uttered for every feeling, emotion, or thought – all was transferred sufficiently with that embrace.

✷✷✷✷✷✷✷✷✷

A few passers-by took brief and casual notice of the couple, but no one had the adequate context to register the significance of the moment, and, therefore, allowed the scene they had witnessed to quickly pass from their thoughts as they went about their business.

And thus, the story ends, just as it took place, unnoticed... perhaps as it should be.

"Life is but a loan to man; death is the creditor who will one day claim it."

Proverbial Sayings and Traditions, pg. 341[89]

Epilogue

The air is unseasonably warm and heavy despite a slight breeze moving in steadily from the northeast. The only recognizable sound of life is that of a small, solitary bird, hopping in quick bursts from branch to branch within a tall mature birch tree, occasionally chirping as it jumps about. As if in impatient anticipation, the bird periodically jerks a glance off toward the horizon in the east, expectant of something.

This humble and simple manifestation of Creation is, and will always remain, completely unaware of the tragic circumstances that befell Existence, threatening its very reality. Its existence will be one of ignorance, but ultimately peaceful in that ignorance.

Suddenly the bird's attention is captured, though it remains focused eastward, showing no discernible signs of adjusting its gaze, with the exception occasionally of a random sideways cock of the neck. Slowly, ever so slowly, a change had begun at the horizon line, a change for which the bird was clearly waiting. The faintest rays of luminescence were gradually appearing. The initial signs of the newly rising sun will remain nothing more than a dull burnt-orange glow for some time before the brilliance of the corona will shyly peek out from behind the horizon. Continuing to stare toward the breaking daylight, the bird remained still, blissfully so, as if instinctively feeding directly from the increasingly powerful waves of light.

Existence was, is, and will ever be. Creation was, is, and will ever be. The cycle of life forever continues upon the arrival of dawn, of Light.

Index

** *Cover* Found in Camille Flammarion's *L'Atmosphère: Météorologie Populaire*, by an anonymous artist, [1888].
1 *Illustration in Jacques Collin de Plancy's Dictionnaire Infernal, by Louis le Breton, [1863].*
2 *Archangel Azrael: Words of Comfort, Wisdom and Illumination, by Dawn Marshall, [2010], self-published.*
3 *Purely fictional reference to the Angel of Death*
4 Also referred to as the Akashic Record, as it is in the ancient Hindu Mahabharata texts, or by modern physicists as the zero-point field.
5 Keres: According to Theoi.com, Keres are the spirits of female demons responsible for devouring souls that perished in an unfavorable way. Keres are further referred to as beings that carry off the souls damned to hell. The Keres are also referred to as Samael's Servitors.
6 Azrael: According to ancient sources Azrael is commonly referred to as the Angel of Death, a figure responsible for ushering the souls of mankind to the afterlife. While there is some disagreement as to whether this being escorts all deceased souls to the afterlife, or just the righteous, he is charged with escorting souls that have passed out of this mortal realm back to the

origins of creation.
7 *Our Name is Melancholy: The Complete Books of Azrael*, by Leilah Wendell, [2002], Westgate Press.
8 *Folk-lore of the Holy Land: Moslem, Christian, and Jewish*, by J.E. Hanauer, [1907], found at sacred-texts.com.
9 *Studies in Islamic Mysticism*, by Reynold A. Nicholson, [1921], found at sacred-texts.com.
10 *Folk-lore of the Holy Land: Moslem, Christian, and Jewish*, by J.E. Hanauer, [1907], found at sacred-texts.com.
11 *The Messages of Azrael: The Archangel's Teachings on Death, Dying and Living Well*, by Catherine Morgan, [2008], Guiding Light Publications.
12 *Archangel Azrael: Words of Comfort, Wisdom, and Illumination*, by Dawn Marshall, [2010], self-published.
13 *Archangel Azrael: Words of Comfort, Wisdom, and Illumination*, by Dawn Marshall, [2010], self-published.
14 *Our Name is Melancholy: The Complete Book of Azrael*, by Leilah Wendell, [2002], Westgate Publishing.
15 *The Messages of Azrael: The Archangel's Teachings on Death, Dying and Living Well*, by Catherine Morgan, [2008], Guiding Light Publications.
16 *Our Name is Melancholy: The Complete Books of Azrael*, by Leilah Wendell, [2002], Westgate Publishing.
17 Hortus deliciarum, by Herrad von Landsberg, [1196].
18 *The Seven Evil Spirits*, translated by R.C. Thompson, [1903], found at http://www.sacred-texts.com/ane/seven.htm.
19 *Our Name is Melancholy: The Complete Books of Azrael*, by Leilah Wendell, [2002], Westgate Press.
20 *Archangel Azrael: Words of Comfort, Wisdom, and Illumination*, by Dawn Marshall, [2010], self-published.
21 Malak al-Mawt is one of the many titles associated with Azrael in the Islamic tradition, https://en.wikipedia.org/wiki/Azrael.
22 In several mythologies of Azrael, he is described as having four thousand wings, seventy thousand feet, and as many eyes and tongues as there are mortal beings, http://www.angelfire.com/de/poetry/Whoswho/Azrael.html.
23 In Greek mythology Thanatos is the angel of death, and generally associated with Azrael in other traditions, https://espressocomsaudade.wordpress.com/2014/08/05/honest-mythis-

lamic-azrael/.
24 *Our Name is Melancholy: The Complete Books of Azrael*, by Leilah Wendell, [2002], Westgate Publishing.
25 *The Messages of Azrael: The Archangel's Teachings on Death, Dying, and Living Well*, by Catherine Morgan, [2008], Guiding Light Publications.
26 *Fictitious & Symbolic Creatures In Art, With Special Reference to Their Use In British Heraldry*, by John Vinycomb, [1906], found at www.sacred-texts.com.
27 *Kabbalah Denudata: The Kabbalah Unveiled*, translated by S.L. Macgregor Mathers, [1912], found at www.sacred-texts.com.
28 *Folk-lore of the Holy Land, Moslem, Christian and Jewish*, by J.E. Hanauer, [1907], found at www.sacred-texts.com.
29 *Archangel Azrael: Words of Comfort, Wisdom, and Illumination*, by Dawn Marshall, [2010], self-published.
30 According to a few stories passed down about Azrael, there is mention that he was once a mortal being that went by the name Azra, and when ordained to serve as an angel of death, he received the honorific of his name, Azra'el, https://espressocomsaudade.wordpress.com/2014/08/05/honest-mythislamic-azrael/.
31 *Archangel Azrael: Words of Comfort, Wisdom, and Illumination*, by Dawn Marshall, [2010], self-published.
32 *Archangel Azrael: Words of Comfort, Wisdom, and Illumination*, by Dawn Marshall, [2010], self-published.
33 britannica.com/topic/Azrael
34 http://www.angelfire.com/de/poetry/Whoswho/Azrael.html
35 britannica.com/topic/Azrael
36 https://en.wikipedia.org/wiki/Azrael
37 *Archangel Azrael: Words of Comfort, Wisdom, and Illumination*, by Dawn Marshall, [2010], self-published.
38 *Our Name is Melancholy: The Complete Books of Azrael*, by Leilah Wendell, [2002], Westgate Publishing.
39 *Our Name is Melancholy: The Complete Books of Azrael*, by Leilah Wendell, [2002], Westgate Publishing.
40 Samael is traditionally referred to as a malicious archangel and in general a source of great evil in such literature Talmudic cosmologies, https://en.wikipedia.org/wiki/Samael.
41 The Grigori have the authority to investigate the Ethereal

Disturbances left behind by deceased mortals for the purpose of interpreting their Echoes there on, www.amadan.org/Innomine/Azrael.htm.

42 The Mercurian have the power to identify the identity of a deceased soul, www.amadan.org/Innomine/Azrael.htm.

43 *The Knight of the Tower* from Geoffroy de La Tour Landry's *Examples of God-Forcht and Inheritability, or the Mirror of Virtue*, by Michael Furter, [1513].

44 *The Kebra Nagast*, by E.A. Wallis Budge, [1932], found at sacred-texts.com.

45 https://en.wikipedia.org/wiki/Keres

46 Tenebrae is the Latin term sometimes used for the Keres in Greek mythology.

47 *Our Name is Melancholy: The Complete Books of Azrael*, by Leilah Wendell, [2002], Westgate Press.

48 *Angel Of Death*, from Conrad Reiter's *Mortilogus*, [1508].

49 *Folk-lore of the Holy Land, Moslem, Christian and Jewish*, by J. E. Hanauer, [1907], found at sacred-texts.com.

50 The "Seraphim Council" was, is, and will be the body of Eternal entities that watch over Existence. Azrael and Samael are among the many Cosmic beings that were, are, and will be ordained to serve the Seraphim Council in some way, http://www.amadan.org/Innomine/Azrael.htm.

51 www.amadan.org/Innomine/Azrael.htm

52 www.amadan.org/Innomine/Azrael.htm

53 https://espressocomsaudade.wordpress.com/2014/08/05/honest-mythislamic-azrael/

54 *Our Name is Melancholy: The Complete Books of Azrael*, by Leilah Wendell, [2002], Westgate Publishing.

55 www.amadan.org/Innomine/Azrael.htm

56 *Our Name is Melancholy: The Complete Books of Azrael*, by Leilah Wendell, [2002], Westgate Publishing.

57 *Our Name is Melancholy: The Complete Books of Azrael*, by Leilah Wendell, [2002], Westgate Publishing.

58 *Ars Moriendi*, artist unknown, [15th century].

59 *Orpheus, Myths of the World*, by Padraic Colum, [1930], found at www.saced-texts.com.

60 Among the several alternative titles associated with Samael in various traditions, have been the "destroyer" or Mashhit, the "accuser", Satan, and "severity of God", https://en.wikipedia.org/

wiki/Samael.
61 *Orpheus, Myths of the World*, by Padriac Colum, [1930], found at www.sacred-texts.com.
62 *Chronicles of Jerahmeel*, by M. Gaster [1899], found at www. sacred-texts.com.
63 https://en.wikipedia.org/wiki/Dumah
64 *Orpheus, Myths of the World*, by Padriac Colum, [1930], found at www.sacred-texts.com.
65 *The Book of Ceremonial Magic*, by Arthur Edward Waite, [1913], found at www. sacred-texts.com.
66 One of the translations of Samael into English is "poison of God", https://en.wikipedia.org/wiki/Samael.
67 britannica.com/topic/Azrael
68 www.amadan.org/Innomine/Azrael.htm
69 *The Forgotten Books of Eden*, by Rutherford H. Platt, Jr., [1926], found at www.sacred-texts.com.
70 www.amadan.org/Innomine/Azrael.htm
71 *From Bible Pictures and What They Teach Us*, by Charles Foster, [1914], A.J. Holmon Co, found at www.sacred-texts.com.
72 *Arabian Nights, the Marvels and Wonders of the Thousand and One Nights*, adapted from Richard F. Burton's Unexpurgated Translation, by Jack Zipes, [1991], Penguin Books, found at www. sacred-texts.com.
73 Resurrection is a widely misunderstood concept. Most people hold, for the most part, a Judeo-Christian perception. That belief follows generally that the souls of beings deemed by God or the Christ figure to be righteous, will, at the Second Coming be reunited with their physical body in its perfect form. This, however, is a misconception, a corruption of the truth over time. Resurrection is the ultimate sacrament undergone by a mortal being, a corporeal entity no longer bound to the cycles of reincarnation. The Energy of Life of those entities that are determined to be righteous is, upon mortal death, translated into a cosmic form, a form ordained in the service of Existence for Eternity.
74 From Georg Weicker's *The soul bird in the old literature and art. A mythological-archaeological investigation*, [1902].
75 *The Appointment in Samarra*, as retold by W. Somerset Maugham, [1933].
76 Natron is a mixture of sodium carbonate decahydrate, so-

dium bicarbonate, and small traces of sodium chloride and sodium sulfate. Natron is traditionally associated with the mummification process of ancient Egypt, https://en.wikipedia.org/wiki/Natron.

77 A sky-cleaver is, according to several mythologies, a large obsidian bladed hand ax that could cleave anything, physical or otherwise, https://forgottenrealms.fandom.com/wiki/Sky_Cleaver#:~:text=Sky%20Cleaver%20was%20a%20massive,-carved%20images%20of%20the%20gods.

78 *Chronicles of Jerahmeel*, by M. Gaster, [1899], found at www.sacred-texts.com.

79 The incantations recited in this chapter are of ancient origins; a derivative thereof can be found in the Book of the Dead, and in the tomb chapel of Rekhmira as part of what is referred by Egyptologists as the "Opening of the Mouth" incantations and protocols. According to Egyptian mythology, the Opening of the Mouth" prayers and accompanying prescribed protocols were necessary in the process of reviving or reincarnating (resurrecting) someone from the dead, https://www.ucl.ac.uk/museums-static/digitalegypt/religion/wpr2.html.

80 *The Book of the Dead*, translated by E.A. Wallis Budge, [1895].

81 This is a made-up reference to the Angel of Death.

82 *The Pyramid Texts*, translated by Samuel A.B. Mercer, [1952], found at https://www.sacred-texts.com.

83 *The Pyramid Texts*, translated by Samuel A.B. Mercer, [1952], found at https://www.sacred-texts.com.

84 According to the Sufi teacher Al-Jili, Azrael appears to the soul in a form provided by its most powerful metaphors, https://en.wikipedia.org/wiki/Azrael.

85 *Our Name is Melancholy: The Complete Books of Azrael*, by Leilah Wendell, [2002], Westgate Publishing.

86 *The Messages of Azrael: The Archangel's Teachings on Death, Dying and Living Well*, by Catherine Morgan, [2008], Guiding Light Publications.

87 *Archangel Azrael: Words of Comfort, Wisdom and Illumination*, by Dawn Marshall, [2010], self-published.

88 *Dance of Death*, by Hans Holbein the Younger, [1538].

89 *Hebraic Literature, Translations from the Talmud Midrashim and* Kabbala, by Maurice H. Harris, [1901], found at www.sacred-texts.com.